SO-BBE-741

THE BRONCO MAN

THE BRONCO MAN

MAN

•

Scott Smith

AVALON BOOKS
NEW YORK

Published by Avalon Books,
an imprint of Thomas Bouregy & Co., Inc.
160 Madison Avenue, New York, NY 10016

Library of Congress Cataloging-in-Publication Data

Smith, Scott, 1923-
   The Bronco man / Scott Smith.
      p.   cm.
   ISBN 978-0-8034-7601-1 (acid-free paper)
1. Ranchers—Wyoming—Fiction.
2. Vendetta—Fiction.   I. Title.
   PS3619.M5935B76 2011
   813'.6—dc22

                              2011005607

PRINTED IN THE UNITED STATES OF AMERICA
ON ACID-FREE PAPER
BY RR DONNELLEY, BLOOMSBURG, PENNSYLVANIA

*To Flois, my wife; Win, my son; Jared, my grandson;
and Ellen, my daughter-in-law;
who shared my thrill of being published*

Chapter One

When Deputy Pete Judd saw the rider searching for the ford to cross Horse Creek at the edge of town, he thought the man was another of Wells Gorman's hired guns, riding in from the Pitchfork range for a day of beer swirling and stud poker at the Horseshoe Saloon.

A panther-slim man of sixty-three, Judd stood behind the murky front window of the sheriff's office, stroking his unshaven chin, watching and wondering where he'd seen the tall man and his big speckled Appaloosa before.

He shifted his weight from one foot to the other. His knees hurt, and both feet ached, and lately he'd been having some trouble with his memory.

It was only when the rider, sitting straight-backed in his saddle, turned the Appaloosa down Six Mile Junction's main street that Judd realized he wasn't one of Wells Gorman's men. He gave thanks for that little favor.

The rider rode at an angle past the sheriff's office. He glanced once over his right shoulder. His eyes found Judd for a second before he looked away.

1

"I know you, mister?" Judd mumbled aloud to himself.

He left the window and crossed the room's oily floor to a gun case in the far corner and removed the Winchester. He pointed the barrel to the ceiling and jacked it once and then returned to stare out the window. The rider had dismounted in front of Delia's Diner and was adjusting the saddle strings on the rear skirts that held a rolled-up tarp.

The longer Judd stared at the man, the more convinced he became that somewhere, sometime in his past, he had been a part of that man's life. The rider, a tall, wide-shouldered man with a slim waist, wore a flat-brimmed black hat pulled low, and as he talked to and patted the large speckled Appaloosa on the neck and flank, Judd noticed a slight hitch to his left leg. Judd caught his breath as he rushed out the front door and stepped onto the boardwalk, his heart beating rapidly.

Limp? Of course!

"Hey, Travis! Wait up there!"

It had been the tail end of a Montana winter at a large rambling ranch house, several men clinging to a large-poled corral, each one cheering as they watched in awed reverence one of their own work a wild horse like no other man could. The horse had shaken with fury; it had leaped and bounded stiff-legged, snapped and slobbered, twisted and swirled, but the man on his back rode him straight-up without pulling leather.

Judd rushed headlong across the street.

Travis Boone paused, turning reluctantly and guardedly, as Judd expected he would, his right hand on the butt of his Walker Colt.

"Well, Pete, how you been?" Boone finally said, in a low

voice that had all the intensity of a line rider on a rainy day. "Good to see you again. Didn't know you were anywhere near Wyoming. I thought you had joined those Chicago Pinkerton boys."

"I gave them a shot, Travis, but they turned me down flat once they found out I'd rode with the Hole in the Wall gang," Judd said. "Just as well, though. I didn't figure I'd get to liking manhunting if I had to hunt my friends." He fell in alongside Boone. "I never thought five years could dull a man's memory," he said. "I didn't recognize you at first, but when I spotted that limp and that big speckled Appaloosa, I knew it had to be you."

Boone smiled. "It happens to most of us. Too many tough old broomtails trying to throw us into the dirt and stomp on us."

"Well, ain't many of them had that kind of luck with you that I know of," Judd said.

Boone stepped up onto the boardwalk in front of Delia's. "I guess there's something good about being recognized, even as a man with soft bones," he said.

"Aw, what th' hey . . . they couldn't cripple you."

"Lately I'm feeling such."

"What's brought you way down here, anyhow? You're a long ways from the Little Rockies! Tell me, how's old Harvey Logan and th' boys these days? What's the Kid been up to lately? Still loving the women and robbing banks and trains, I allow."

"Not as much as in the past. Right now he's in a Knoxville jail waiting for Pinkerton detective Lowell Spence to identify him," Boone said, as he stepped through the restaurant door.

Judd jutted his chin toward a table up against the wall on their right, and motioned to a heavy blond woman behind the counter whacking batter in a large crockery bowl with a wooden spoon.

"Coffee over here, Delia. Two cups."

"Be right with you, Deputy. Anything else you like?"

"Breakfast will do it fine. How about your house special? Biscuits, two eggs, sausage, and two syrupy pancakes for each of us—put both on my tab."

"Coming right up."

Boone said, "I'll pay my own ticket, Pete." He'd never ordered a breakfast that big, though, and he wondered about the cost of two eggs, sausages, pancakes, and biscuits. His plan was not to go through all his money on his first meal in two days.

"It's my privilege," Judd said sharply, fingering his deputy's badge. "I'm the law in Six Mile Junction, you know. Besides, I can't remember the last time one of my friends came by so we could talk a spell."

While they waited for Delia to rustle up two large white plates and thick white coffee cups, Judd wanted to know what had brought Travis to Wyoming. "You looking for somebody, Travis? Maybe I can give you a hand if you are. Not many folks around here that I don't know by first name. Somebody owe you, an' you're wanting to be paid?"

Boone looked around the diner and wagged his head. "Nope. Nothing like that. You could say I'm about as close to riding the grub-line as an out-of-work bronco man can get."

Judd stared at him. "You're wha—?"

"I'm out of work."

"How long has that been?"

"Couple months now."

"Are you telling me Bill Yates let you go?"

"That's what he did. He gave me a month's wages an' said he was sorry as all get-out."

For a few moments, Judd and Boone nursed the coffee Delia had placed before them and stared blankly at the clean tabletop. Judd fiddled with his fork and seemed to be considering something. "You know something, Travis? There's a whole lot of things in this blame old world we live in today that I finally learned to figure out, but when it comes to Bill Yates letting you go, that's way above my bend. Don't he know you're the best bronco man that ever flung a saddle on a horse? He'll look a long time before he finds another like you."

Boone shrugged. "He told me that 'most every day."

Delia brought their breakfast to the table, smoothed out the tablecloth, placed the plates of sausage and eggs and flapjacks in front of them, then issued her own opinion about life in Wyoming. "Jobs are scarce as hens' teeth these days," she said with authority. "I don't know of any rancher in Wyoming other than that Wells Gorman what has any opening for even a stray dog, much less a man what needs steady work like your friend here does."

Pete shifted slightly in his chair and looked up at Delia. "Aw, c'mon, Delia, there's always a place to lay your head if you look long enough."

"You just name me one. Just one," she said, flaring a little.

"Okay. How about the Double Deuce? You ain't forgetting that little lady out there in the river country, are you? She could use a good man like my friend here if she wasn't so blame timid of strangers."

"Oh, sure, Mary Agnes Canfield! Why, of course! Why didn't I figure you'd remember her? That red-haired widow's caused more heartburn in these parts than my cooking."

Judd grinned at her. "Yep, I think you're right about that."

"Of course, you know, her being a widow may come to an end right soon. I guess you've heard how she's about to be wed up one of these days," Delia said grumpily.

"No, I ain't heard that. Wed? To who?"

"Wells Gorman. He's had his eye on her ever since the day her husband got himself shot dead."

"Yeah, well, I've heard something of that, but—nope, that ain't happening."

"Humph!" Delia said, "Ain't no *but*s about it, not where Wells Gorman stands. You know when there's anything worth wanting and Wells Gorman wants it, it'd take the backhand of God to keep him from getting it."

Boone had been listening closely. When the waitress walked back to the counter, he asked Judd, "Tell me about this Gorman feller you been mentioning. Is he hiring?"

Judd sighed. He watched Boone's face as he said, "Gorman's a wealthy man, Travis. He hires and buys 'most anything he wants, and when he can't buy it up, he takes it. The man has a large spread called the Pitchfork; it's just south of the Double Deuce . . . no family life. They say he's Wyoming's richest bachelor. I was about to mention him to you, but he only hires the kind of man who's selling his gun." Judd cleared his throat. "I didn't figure you'd fit in with that bunch, since—"

Boone shrugged indifferently. "Who knows? I haven't had much of a chance of fitting in anywhere lately," he said, holding Judd in a cool, sober gaze. "But I'd like to hear more about this lady rancher you and that cook lady mentioned."

"That'd be Mary Agnes Canfield. She owns a nice little ranch along the South Fork of the Licking River. She's a widow. Right now Wells and her are in a little spat over some land and water she owns, but that don't mean a man should let her problems with Gorman turn him away from the gate. Woman needs help—that's a pure fact—and here you are, a man in need of a job. Most men around these parts would give up an eyetooth for one day's work at the Deuce."

Judd smiled lazily. "Course, I don't know how you'd feel taking orders from a woman who has such a strict conviction of what's right and what's wrong, especially since you spent all that time busting horses for old Bill Yates. I do hear she's a fine cook, though."

Boone locked eyes with the deputy. "Well, I'm fair game," he confessed.

"Okay, then. The Double Deuce is about five or six hundred acres—small when compared to the Pitchfork—but she has the finest graze this side of Texas . . . and she has all the water she will ever need with the South Fork running through her range. That's something Wells Gorman don't have, but anything's possible, I guess." Judd shoved his chair back from the table and stood. "Who knows? She might take a liking to your old rustic hide and hire you right there on the spot, but if she did, you would need to take the advice of an old peckerwood who knows there's a mean, mean side to Wells Gorman. He surely wouldn't like hearing that."

"What's he got to do with her hiring me?"

"You're a man, ain't you? That's enough to give Gorman the only reason he needs to get you into a gunfight. He'll want you on the move before you get your first night's sleep. He's been trying for years to get one of his men hired by

Mary Agnes, but she knows it's the South Fork water he wants."

"So?"

"He'll see you as someone she hired to look him in the eye and dare him to put a hand on the butt of his gun. If I know Wells right, the first thing he'll do is send five or six of his best men to see if you've got any sand in your belly. So before you get your saddle into her bunkhouse, you need to give it your best thought. Is it worth being beat to a pulp or shot at just for a winter at her ranch?"

"That bad, huh?"

"Well, it's happened before, and it's likely to happen again."

"Not to me, it won't." Boone had heard all he needed to about Wells Gorman and his nasty ways; it sounded to Boone as though Wells Gorman was not only rich, but he thought a hell of a lot of himself—a big man with money who thought it was his God-given right to run roughshod over anyone who had something he wanted.

"How about the lady?" Boone asked.

"What about her?"

"What's she like?"

"I've got some thoughts on her. That is, if you're interested."

"Let's hear them."

"I've got a better idea. How about you and me ride out there so you can decide on your own hook? Seems to me that'd solve a lot of your wondering. She'll look at you, and you can take a look at her."

Boone smiled as he stood up. "What're we waiting on?"

Chapter Two

Well, here we are. Didn't take near as long as I thought it would," Deputy Judd said, reining up. The sun was still high but without any warmth. Boone and Judd had just ridden out of the timber shadows onto a wide, rocky plot of ground that overlooked a valley heavy with sun-cured buffalo grass and a thick growth of willow trees being fed by the South Fork.

Boone reined his Appaloosa to a stop and looked out over the valley to see an impressive, low-roofed building with a pole corral and a lone horse.

"I need to ask you a personal question before I ride out of here," Pete Judd said, clearing his throat.

Boone laughed. "I thought everything you asked me was personal, but don't let that stop you."

Judd was unable to repress a slow grin. "Well, when Mary Agnes gets around to asking you about your past, what do you plan on telling her?"

Boone looked at Judd, somewhat startled. "The *truth,* Pete, what else?" he said forcefully.

9

"I figured that would be your answer, but what *part* of the truth are we talking about?"

"My six years in the Little Rockies as a bronco man for the Rafter K."

"Okay, then, what if she looks at that Walker Colt on your hip and that fast-draw holster you've worn thin and asks about your *other* life?"

Boone shot Judd a sideways glance, his gray eyes showing concern. "Now, you know that part of my life is behind a closed door, Pete. Has been for over six years. Maybe she won't ask."

"Oh, she'll ask, all right. Believe you me. What I'm saying is, she won't come right out and say it, but she's not fond of any man who has a reputation as a gunfighter—and especially not a man who once actually *was* a gunfighter. To her way of thinking, those kinds of men have a way of dying sudden-like."

"Well, that's out of my hands, Pete. If she'd rather hire a man with an empty holster, then she'll need to look elsewhere."

His face marked with grim humor, Judd said, "That's about what I expected to hear." He swung his horse around and urged it up the small slope at a gallop, a concerned frown on his face. He paused at the top long enough to twist his body around in the saddle and watched Boone splash across the small creek on his way to the Double Deuce ranch house.

He shook his head and muttered to himself, "I don't know if I've done you a good turn or got you killed."

Boone rode up to the wide front porch of the Canfield ranch house alone, expecting little. On the yonder side of the house he noticed a windmill, a bunkhouse, and a pole corral next to a red-roofed barn.

The strong scent of brewing coffee hung in the air. That meant someone was inside, and it could also mean that whoever it was wasn't sending out invitations.

"Hello the house," he called.

He heard the latch being thrown quickly and watched the heavy front door ease open a small crack, just large enough for a double-barreled shotgun to poke through.

A soft, feminine voice followed. "Whoever you are, mister, I want *both* hands on that saddle horn plain enough to see the veins. You need to know that this shotgun has a hair trigger and couldn't miss that big Appaloosa you're sitting on."

"I believe you, ma'am." Boone didn't doubt for a minute she would pull the trigger if he made a move she didn't think was necessary. What was it Pete had said? Something about her aversion to guns? Yet here she was, threatening to blow him out of the saddle with no hesitation in her voice.

Boone raised his right hand from the smooth Walker butt and placed it on top of his left hand. Both hands now rested on the saddle horn, with the reins tightly gripped.

"I, uh—" He started as the door opened soundlessly and she stepped out onto the porch.

A red-haired woman in faded denim pants and a well-fitting plaid shirt stood there, shotgun leveled in his direction, looking at him with the biggest blue eyes he had ever seen. She was not too tall, maybe five-seven, and was not gaunt from hard labor, as most ranch women he'd met were. She was at least in her late thirties, but Boone could see why any man would ride a far piece just to have a long look at her. He enjoyed what he saw standing before him, and he wondered if she could see that in his gray eyes.

She gazed at him for a long while before saying in a testy voice, "What is it you want, mister?"

"Morning, ma'am," Boone said. "I'm really sorry to give you a fright this early in the morning, but I—"

"Don't worry, you didn't give me a fright."

He removed his hat and tried to smile without showing his delight. *No wonder Wells Gorman wants to stay on her good side,* he thought—*this is one beautiful woman.*

"A thousand pardons, ma'am," Boone said, his voice low and soft, as was his Kentucky nature. "I'd sure feel much better if you lowered that ten-gauge a bit, ma'am. It'd sure cure my breathing problem."

She didn't lower it, but her reply was polite. "I asked you a question, mister. What do you want?"

"Well, ma'am, I'm the kind of man who likes to do first things first, if you don't mind. I'm not too keen on talking with a shotgun pointed at my belly. I hope you've figured that out."

She clearly wasn't concerned with his wishes. The shotgun did not move.

"I was told you needed some help over the winter, ma'am. Of course, if that's not the case, then if you'll allow me, I'll just turn this big ol' horse of mine around, and I'll ride on like I had first planned on doing."

"Just who told you I needed help?"

"A deputy sheriff over in Six Mile Junction mentioned it to me, ma'am. He rode out here partway with me and showed me how to get down off that big hill to your ranch house without being shot. This *is* the Double Deuce, ain't it, ma'am?"

Softly she said, "Yes, it is." She pushed away from the wall and walked out to stand on the edge of the porch, continuing to give him the once-over. What her sky-blue eyes found was a man with some humor in his gray eyes. His was a strong face, and not all that bad looking, with a stubborn chin that had been shaved clean, and wide and thick shoulders. He wore a heavy sheepskin coat, a denim shirt, and shotgun chaps. The denim shirt, she noticed, had seen some long years of wear and tear.

She said, "Well, do you have a name?"

"Yes, ma'am. My name is Travis Alexander Boone."

"Where you from, Mr. Boone?"

"Montana."

"You born there?"

"No, ma'am. I'm Kentucky born and reared," he said.

"Pete Judd thinks he knows more about me than he really does, but I admit he's right this time. I do happen to be in need of some help." She lowered the shotgun to her side. "You can relax, Mr. Boone. My name is Canfield—Mary Agnes Canfield."

"That's a real nice name, ma'am."

"Thank you."

He admired the shine her red hair gave off and the sound of her voice, and he thought how she would have looked far better if she had welcomed him with the warm smile she now wore, rather than the snout of a double-barreled shotgun. He still wondered whether he had heard Pete Judd correctly. The shotgun in her hands seemed to fit quite well. Maybe it was true that Pete didn't know as much about her as he thought he did.

"Have you ever worked a ranch, Mr. Boone?"

"Yes, ma'am, I surely have," he said with haste, remembering what Pete had said about her way of probing for a clear look into a man's past. She continued to watch him as though she was expecting a long, drawn-out tale of deception. When he didn't give her one, she asked him, "You mind telling me where that was?"

He said, "Until three months ago I was the head bronco peeler for the Rafter K up in Montana's Little Rockies. You've heard of the Rafter K, I'm sure."

"Yes, I've heard of the Rafter K."

"Well, it was my home and bed for six good years. Before that I spent some time riding for Teddy Blue, protecting his cattle and his reputation, did some hunting in the Big Snowy Mountains, some in the Wolf Mountains, besides lots of other places and things, mostly fence repairing, branding work, and bog riding when it became absolutely necessary—that sort of cowboy thing."

There. She almost smiled. A dimple deepened. Just then, she was as warm and sweet looking as a woman could ever be; no frown, just a handsome woman by all accounts.

"And you left all that for Wyoming?" she said. "Too many winters, I suppose?"

"Well, no, not exactly, ma'am, but I've got to be honest with you: Last winter almost took all the starch out of my bones. It was one of those winters Montana seems to have every once in a while, especially up there in the Big Snowy Mountains. It snowed and blew so hard, it froze all the chickens to the side of a woodshed." He paused. "But the truth be, I rode out when my boss up and sold all two thousand acres he had to some men from Chicago who turned the Rafter K into a *dude* ranch of sorts. Lots of people showed up, but most of them didn't know that Montana was part of the United States. A lot of them thought they were in Canada."

"Did Pete mention anything about a few cattle we bought last month, Mr. Boone?"

"No, ma'am."

"I have a small bunch I bought, close to a hundred. They're penned up in Six Mile waiting for us to bunch them up and get them on the trail. They have to be driven around Broken Hand Wells and on through the gap south of Bannock Rock before making it to our south graze. It's quite a ways . . . and a little risky, with all the rustlers that have been working in our territory lately. If you're in no big hurry to be on your way to Cheyenne, or wherever you planned to ride, maybe you could wait around for my son, Hoke, to return to give you some help. He's off looking for strays but should return before long."

Boone was surprised. He hesitated. "Is that an offer, ma'am?"

"Yes, it is."

"Well, I could certainly do that, ma'am," Boone said, pleased to get in a word. "I'd be mighty thankful. A man like me needs a lot of work to keep his mind from going stale, especially with winter coming and all the stuff the cold brings with it."

She sighed with mock exasperation and stared at him a little longer, her sky-blue eyes wandering down to the big shiny Walker Colt on his right hip. Despite herself, she was beginning to like the looks of the man, but she detested the sight of the gun he carried. She gazed with interest at the way the gun and holster hung on his slim hip. Obviously he knew what it was there for and how to use it if it became necessary. Her husband, Creed, had known about guns.

And he'd died for it.

She had the sense to know the worth of a gun, just as she did the saddle and the spur, but some men carried guns for the wrong reason. She'd met many of them. She still remembered the emptiness she'd felt when her husband was brought to her doorstep, lying quietly in the bed of a stranger's wagon, strewn with hay and fresh blood and with a bullet in his back.

A bullet in the back! Such cowardice.

Still, there was no use wondering about Travis Alexander Boone until she could find out whether he was who he said he was. She didn't relish spending the winter with a man who sold his gun to the highest bidder, if that was what Boone usually did. She took in the dusty black hat he had replaced on his head of long black hair, which strayed below the brim and curled within inches of his wide shoulders, and finally raised her gaze back to the clear gray eyes that held hers without wavering.

She also noticed the bone-handled bowie knife he carried in a sheath in his left boot and shivered at the thought of his burying it in a man's flesh.

"I don't mean to be blunt, Mr. Boone, but I hope you're not running from the law, or anything such as that."

"No, ma'am. I don't do a lot of running from much of anything. I'm exactly what you see. There ain't much more," he said. "There may be things you won't like about me, but one thing you won't have to be concerned with, ma'am: If you ever get to where I need to ride for somewhere else, that's what I'll do. You have my word on that."

She hesitated for a moment and said, "I'm ashamed to have asked such a thing, Mr. Boone. Please forget I brought it up."

"I'm okay with that. It was the right thing for you to do."

"Okay, then, you'll find the bunkhouse to be clean. There's a water basin inside and fresh towels. When you're settled, if you like, we'll have a cup of coffee and some doughnuts I made while we wait for Hoke to return."

Boone nodded. Maybe his lousy luck was beginning to turn the corner in his direction—maybe it was something close to divine intervention, whatever that was.

He dismounted and started to lead the big Appaloosa toward the bunkhouse.

Mary Agnes stopped him. "Would you wait just a second, Mr. Boone? I need to explain something to you."

"That's not necessary, ma'am."

"Hoke and I have made it this far since his father was killed. This may sound a bit eccentric to you, Mr. Boone, but what I mean is, I'm not on the market for a man's affections. I'd like that understood, so there are no bruised feelings."

Boone didn't reply. *I'll swear,* he thought, *if that don't hobble your horse, nothing will.* She had just informed him he was a hired hand and nothing more.

"My husband's been dead two years," she said.

"I'm sorry about that, ma'am."

"I am too, but there's men in Six Mile who think a woman like me without a man about is a helpless little soul who doesn't know the difference between a double rig and a horn-string. That's not the case."

Boone nodded. "I understand that, ma'am."

He led the Appaloosa to the bunkhouse and tethered him to a snubbing post in front. For the life of him, he couldn't recall anything he had said that would have made her think he was looking for something more than a winter job. *What kind of man does she think I am?*

At least he would be working again, if no longer than a

few weeks of winter. Sometimes things had a way of changing right before a person's eyes. Who knew what another
day of conversation and a long winter might have to offer?

Mary Agnes remained on the porch. She watched Travis
Alexander Boone dismount and pat his horse on the neck,
and she waited to see if he would turn around. She smiled
when he did and went back into the house.

Chapter Three

Eighteen-year-old Hoke Canfield heard Turkey Adams yelling out that Eagle Pass was infested with wagons and men with digging equipment. Another wagon carried a sign on its broadside: CAUTION, DYNAMITE.

"Looks like they're planning to blow a hole in that riverbank," Turkey called out to Hoke. "We better slow 'em down! They done tore that barbwire fence Mary Agnes strung up between those two ridges wide open. Ripped it right out of the ground."

Turkey was pointing to the ridge of land as Hoke reined up beside him. "They can't do that, Hoke! If they blow a hole in that hillside, they'll wash your dad right out of the ground and all the way to Gorman's reservoir! We better get down there an' scatter 'em like the bunch of buzzards they are."

Hoke waved his rifle over his head. "Let's go get 'em!"

Hoke had forgotten he had given his mother his word he'd make it back to the Double Deuce long before nightfall. He had learned to despise men like the ones around those wagons, and he wasn't about to let this opportunity escape unchallenged. What those men were doing just wasn't right. *A man works hard, sometimes all his life, doing every damn thing he can do to build a place fit for him and his family to live like honest folk, then here comes a bunch of scum doing whatever they can to ruin everything in sight.*

Turkey beat Hoke to the rim of the ridge. Below them they heard shouts of warning.

"We better look out!" Hoke yelled. "There's more coming out of them trees."

Turkey broke hard to the left, fired several times downhill, and punished his horse with a hard rake of spur that sent the startled animal into a dead run, away from Hoke. Turkey was using his hat for encouragement, slapping it against the rump of his horse. Just then the men with rifles began jacking and firing at Turkey as if they aimed to rip him to shreds.

"Take 'em out, Turkey!" Hoke yelled, and he almost gutted his own horse with a rake of his spurs.

Turkey was shouting and motioning for Hoke to hunker down, as the two of them stormed off the top of the ridge and went soaring over the rim, sending a flurry of shots in every direction. At the same time, two men using a wagon as shelter had their rifle levers working, scattering lead in every direction. Rocks and shavings of dried tree limbs flew about like a raging winter ice storm.

Suddenly Turkey yelled, "I'm hit bad, Hoke!" He was flat on the ground with an ugly belly wound, his arms out. His horse continued to run, empty stirrups flapping.

As Hoke spun his horse around, he was nicked in his shooting arm. Grasping his arm, he struck out for a small pile of malpais rock, shooting left-handed as he rode. With a quick glance at the three riders charging for cover behind a downed tree, Hoke whipped his horse to the safe side of the ridge, just below the rim.

From there he was out of their sight, safe at least for a while.

The shooting continued from the two who were now drawing a host of friends from beyond the trees. Two more men began peppering the ground all around Hoke, who was suddenly out of the saddle and having one hell of a time clinging to his horse's reins with one hand while shooting aimlessly with the other, hitting nothing except the air over the men's heads.

At the same time, a man in a long red coat homed in on Hoke with renewed vengeance. Dozens of well-placed bullets began spraying the ground around him. Hoke's horse, a spotted Colorado Ranger, went walleyed and stiff-legged, straining Hoke's grip on the reins.

Hoke knew that the longer he fought his horse, the better chance he'd catch a bullet. He dropped the reins so he could steady his shooting arm. Taking aim, he spotted a man crouched in the bed of a wagon. Hoke sent four shots down the slope, all close with splinters flying, but was unable to keep the shooter pinned down there and watched as he was picked up by a charging rider, who swung his horse madly around the rear gate of the wagon, grabbed the man's arm, and practically dragged him feet-first over the sideboards and onto the horse's rump.

Still shooting, Hoke sent a tall, gangly man with wide chaps flapping and stumbling beneath a wagon, while another man broke and ran to his horse, then disappeared into the trees.

Hoke dismounted and made himself as small as he could against the ground. Hot lead was closing in on him, dirt flying and stinging him with rock fragments, forcing him to crawl behind a larger hillside rock.

He'd have to hope for the best, now. But if he remained where he was, he'd wind up with more holes than his mother's corn-meal sieve. If he rose one more inch—

A shot rang out.

He felt the throb of the bullet. His head slumped forward, his pistol dangling loose in his hand, still warm to the touch. Somewhere men were yelling. "That's it, Solly. Now you're really in trouble. You shot the Canfield boy! Gorman will have your head for that! We better git!"

"Gorman ain't gonna find out."

"You're crazy if you think that."

Hoke knew he was in the worst pickle of his life. Red streaked down his right arm and bled from high on his chest. He put a fistful of dirt on the chest wound to stop the bleeding. If he stayed out here, he'd be a dead man, soon to be covered with shovels full of dirt instead.

He could still hear men yelling, but their voices were fading. He thought he heard the clop of a horse moving about, close, and saddle leather squeaking. Somewhere above him a rifle spouted methodically. Farther off, a man yelled, and horses bolted.

It wasn't Turkey. That much he knew. He had seen Turkey die.

Hoke sighed deeply and closed his eyes to the growing darkness, his final thought of his mother. She would give him a good dressing-down for getting himself shot—he knew that much, at least.

Chapter Four

Travis Boone woke earlier than usual and lay on the soft bed, thinking. If this was going to be the beginning of another long, cold winter riding a fence line and nursing a bunch of smelly cows or mending fences, he'd have to bear with it. See it through to the end.

Surely he could make it through the winter.

Actually, when he thought about it, there was no reason for his lousy mood. He had a decent place to sleep, dry and warm, a place to eat, and a boss a hell of a lot better-looking than Bill Yates, so what else could a man need?

He washed up, shaved, combed his long hair straight back, made sure his fingernails were clean, buttoned up his denim shirt, and shook and brushed his sheepskin coat clean of trail dust and any small varmints that might have made a nest there. The thin spots of wear on the elbows couldn't be helped. One of these days he'd find a store-bought coat that would fit his wide shoulders as well as his money pouch. But first he'd need a payday or two.

He could smell breakfast on the table when he reached

the main house and knocked on the door. His stomach was ready. Mary Agnes opened the door and welcomed him in and to a table laden with a stack of pancakes, sausage, scrambled eggs, steaming coffee, and a bowl of redeye gravy.

"Please have a seat," she said softly. "Leave the door open, so I can see Hoke when he arrives. He should be coming home soon."

Boone felt good to be invited to something this fine. Had he found a gold mine, it couldn't provide a better feeling than sitting across the table from Mary Agnes Canfield.

"My husband, Creed, used to have eggs and pancakes every morning before he'd lift a hand at any kind of work," Mary Agnes said, without looking up from her plate.

"Well, ma'am, I'd say your husband and me have a lot in common," Boone said. "An appreciation of good food and a pretty woman."

What the hell was that? he wondered.

She ignored his remark. "I'm sorry, but I really miss him, Mr. Boone. It's like a giant hole grew in my heart when that happened to him."

He noticed that her lips seemed to quiver slightly when she spoke of her husband. "I can understand that, ma'am."

What a bubblehead! He'd only been on the Deuce one night, and already he'd turned from a man looking for work into a blithering idiot over a blue-eyed, red-haired woman. If he could have, he would've stuck a sock into his mouth and zipped it shut.

"I'm sorry, ma'am . . . I didn't mean anything by what I said."

She smiled. "Oh, I know that, Mr. Boone."

He took a second to taste the first scrambled egg he'd had

in over a year and then asked, "Your husband, was he from some other part of the West, ma'am?"

"No. He was a cut-and-dried New Orleans native, but he thought he should have been born out here, on the plains, or the mountains—anywhere as long as it was the West. Having this ranch was his dream come true," she added. "Creed had a fine law practice back in New Orleans, but all he talked about was living on a ranch, raising some cattle, and wearing a gun on his hip like he was a man born to roam. Freedom, he called it."

Boone didn't think it necessary for Mary Agnes to tell him the ups and downs of her personal life, although he was pleased she'd carried her husband's dreams into her conversation. That was a sign of a good woman, he reckoned.

"I'm sure this is not the same, ma'am, me being here like this."

"What's not the same, Mr. Boone?"

"You having breakfast with the hired help, ma'am."

"Oh, I'm sorry, Mr. Boone. Really, sometimes I talk way too much. Out here we're simply man and woman."

"There's nothing to be sorry for, ma'am—nothing at all."

She shook her head. Not another word was said until she had gone to the kitchen for the coffeepot and brought it with her to the table.

Sipping her coffee, she looked at him and said, "I seem to have lost my appetite, Mr. Boone. My mind's been on Hoke all morning. The boy has never done this before. He's been late quite often, like most young men who think they know what they're doing, but he's always come home before this."

"Where do you think he might be? If you want, I'll—"

"Thank you," she interrupted him. "I'm sure he's fine . . . but mothers do worry, you know. Even when their son is eighteen."

After breakfast, Boone returned to the bunkhouse. It had been a strange night for him, sleeping in the small, empty bunkhouse, warm as a bed tick. There were no unmade bunks, other than his own, which he now made up. No grumbling and cussing men playing cards and telling lies or standing around waiting his turn at the water trough.

It was very unusual.

Every ranch he knew had ranch hands. He wondered what had really happened to the men who once worked here and slept here. There were a dozen empty bunk beds. Pete had said that Wells Gorman and his men made working for the Double Deuce a difficult job. Mary Agnes had mentioned nothing about any trouble she had with Gorman or anybody else. She didn't seem to be worrying over the fact she was shorthanded, although he had a guess her concern over her son wouldn't be settled until he was back at her kitchen table, which was her right.

Her son was obviously young, and probably headstrong, and could be lost, as far as he knew. But Boone's instincts told him that if Mary Agnes Canfield wanted him found, she'd do it herself, and the sooner he understood that, the better it would be for him, or he'd be on the road again.

Looks like you'd better learn your place, Travis Boone, he told himself, and he left the bunkhouse, leading the Appaloosa with him. It was time to give the six hundred acres a once-over. Maybe he'd ride over and take a look at the South Fork too.

A few minutes later, while he was double-checking his pommel bags and bedroll, he heard a man's voice coming from somewhere up in front of the main building, near the front porch.

He finished tying his bedroll behind the saddle and led the Appaloosa a few more feet out from the bunkhouse, where he saw three men sitting on their horses in front of the porch. Mary Agnes stood on the porch, her arms crossed.

"Good morning, Mrs. Canfield," one of the men said.

"What can I do for you?" she asked.

"My name is Alvin Albertson," the man answered, and he touched the brim of his hat with his left hand. He was well dressed, in a clean blue shirt and a calfskin jacket over thin shoulders.

Mary Agnes kept her arms crossed. "I know who you are," she said coldly.

Boone's Appaloosa scuffed the ground with his right front hoof, a nervous habit the horse had when standing around waiting for something to happen.

Albertson must have heard the Appaloosa. He looked away from Mary Agnes just in time to see Boone walk over to stand by the corner of the porch, his horse patiently at his side. A rifle was cradled in Boone's arms.

Albertson's dark face was suddenly intense. It was obvious to Boone the man was bothered by him standing in plain sight near the wide porch.

Albertson removed his hat, showing a retreating hairline. "Mrs. Canfield, I'm president and owner of Irrigations Unlimited, over in Lincoln, Nebraska. I took it on myself to come by this morning so we could discuss in detail some of the early surveying work we'll be doing over yonder at Eagle Pass. I would prefer we do our talking somewhere in private."

"I know who hired you, Mr. Albertson, and I know why," she said bluntly. "And th—"

"Well, that's good to hear, ma'am. I was told you were an extremely cautious woman to deal with and would like to know all the details of what we have in mind. I'd say that's a prudent thing for a woman alone to be in a time such as we live in nowadays."

"What else have you been told, Mr. Albertson?" she asked in her most sardonic voice.

Albertson leaned forward in his saddle, his hands resting on the saddle horn. Boone thought he looked put off by her manner. "As I said—that is, if you don't mind, Mrs. Canfield—I'd like for our conversation to be a private matter, maybe over a cup of coffee," the man said quietly. "Would you consider that, Mrs. Canfield?"

Boone heard her chilly answer and grinned.

"No, Mr. Albertson, this is as private as you'll get. I've had my coffee for the day. So get on with it."

This again caught Albertson by surprise. He looked around and gave Boone a brief glance. "Is she joking?" he asked him with a forced smile.

Boone didn't answer. He only shook his head, while closely observing the two hard-eyed men sitting in their saddles on the yonder side of Albertson's dun horse. Both men were armed with two shiny-holstered Colts each and seemed to be studying him intently. He didn't recall seeing them before, but he knew the kind of men they were.

Alvin Albertson tried once again. "Did I say something wrong, Mrs. Canfield?" His chin twitched as he spoke. He was aware that Boone's attention was on his men now and that his presence was beginning to concern both of them. They were out of position, and, judging by their body language, they knew it.

"Uh . . . I'd like to explain some things to Mrs. Canfield, if you don't mind," he said to Boone.

Boone shrugged. "I have no problem."

Albertson turned back to Mary Agnes. "Again, may we talk inside your house, ma'am? I'd appreciate it very much if what I have to say is just between the two of us. I'd hope you understand."

"Oh, I understand, Mr. Albertson. My house is not in order for company. It's still early in the day. And if it's about your men digging a canal on my land, there's absolutely no need for us to talk. It's not going to happen."

"Oh, I'm sorry, ma'am, but that doesn't matter. We have the right of way—"

"You have nothing of the kind," she said.

"But we do—"

Boone stepped away from the corner of the house. His voice was soft and dry as he raised his eyes to Albertson. "She said you were wrong, Mr. Albertson. You must have misunderstood her."

Albertson stiffened, and his eyes flared. "What was that?"

"I said, maybe you didn't hear the lady. She said you were wrong."

"What's that mean?"

"It sounds to me as if it's time for you to ride out of here."

"Now wait just a minute. I thought—" He started to throw a leg over the saddle and dismount but thought better when he saw Boone aim the barrel of his rifle in his direction.

"I—I'm sorry," Albertson said, and he settled back into his saddle. Boone could see anger scorching the man's narrow face, and he took a step closer to the porch so he was positioned with the three intruders bunched close together.

All he had to do was shoot one and then swing his rifle to the next one and the next. That wouldn't take much effort.

Mary Agnes cleared her throat. Boone looked around. She was standing very stiffly on the porch edge, close enough for her to hear him breathe. "You want me to stay around for a while, ma'am?" His expression was dogged, his gray eyes hard on Albertson and his men.

"Yes, I do," she said.

Albertson seemed to shudder, and he asked, "Is this man a hired gun, Mrs. Canfield? If he is, we'll be riding off once we've had our talk. I've not had much experience with gunfighters."

"Oh, I don't think he's just a gunfighter, Mr. Albertson, but since you're wondering, you might ask *him*. He's probably wondering why you brought two men with you who don't appear to be a pair of company bookkeepers."

Boone guessed Albertson was about finished, yet, like a good, experienced salesman, he gave it one more try. "I'm very sorry, ma'am, I really am. There seems to be some kind of misunderstanding."

"What kind was that, Mr. Albertson?"

"Frankly, ma'am, I rode out here under the impression that our deal had been discussed long beforehand. Fact is, I was plainly given the impression there would be no problem. I was to start work on the canal in a day or so. All I'm doing, ma'am, is my job. I came here to let you know our plans for the canal I am to dig. From what I've been told, and this is my personal opinion, you're missing the chance to invest in a plan that could enhance your future and that of the Double Deuce."

Mary Agnes' expression showed her disapproval. "Just

whom did you discuss it with before you rode up here, Mr. Albertson?" she asked.

"Your neighbor, of course. Wells Gorman, ma'am," Albertson replied.

"That was your first mistake."

"How's that?"

"Gorman doesn't own a blade of grass growing on Eagle Pass, and not only does he not own a single blade, he never will as long as I'm alive."

"Obviously you haven't talked with Mr. Gorman lately."

"You're right. And I don't intend to talk with him, Mr. Albertson. The land he wants to spade up belongs to the Deuce, not the Pitchfork. He's to keep his men off it."

Albertson took a deep breath and stared at Boone, then lowered his eyes and looked back at Mary Agnes. "My thinking is, Mrs. Canfield, you'll be sorry you feel that way. Mr. Gorman needs the water, and I think he intends to have it, one way or the other. The law will be in his favor, I've been told. It's my understanding that he plans to sell off portions of his land for a new settlement down there."

Mary Agnes shrugged. "As long as it's on the Pitchfork."

"I don't believe you understand, ma'am, " Albertson said. "Irrigation is absolutely necessary, and financially it could be very beneficial to both you and Mr. Gorman in the very near future. As it now stands, a canal to distribute water for farming is important. The canal would run through open ditches. There'd be no need for laterals on your land—"

"I have a question," Mary Agnes interrupted.

"Yes?"

"What is it going to take for you to understand that we're through talking?"

"I'm sorry, I just don't understand why."

"It's very simple, Mr. Albertson. Nobody digs a canal on my land. And not that my reasoning is any of your business, but my husband is *buried* down there. Wells Gorman knows that. The South Fork was my husband's favorite fishing spot. He'll not be moved."

Albertson backed up his dun a few feet, shifted his body in the saddle, and turned to Boone, saying, "I have a strong feeling that before this is all over with, we'll be seeing each other on yet another day."

"You could be right, sir," said Boone.

Albertson paused, then frowned at Boone. "Maybe the next time we meet, the conditions will be different."

Boone nodded. "There's always that chance, Mr. Albertson," he said evenly. "But I don't expect the conditions to change."

Albertson looked around, took up the reins of his horse, and motioned for the two men to follow as he rode off.

Looking back, he saw Boone staring at him, and he turned his head and motioned his men to close up ranks. "Do either of you two know that gentleman back there?" he asked, jutting his chin at Boone. Both men twisted in their saddles to peer past Albertson at Boone. Both nodded.

"Yes," one of the men said. "I believe I've seen him before, Mr. Albertson. Yes, sir, I think his name is Alex Boone. He was younger back then. It was Kansas, I believe—maybe Montana."

"Are you and Arch comparable with the likes of him?"

There was no hesitation in their answer.

"I'd say no, we're not, Mr. Albertson," the second man said. "And I don't know any of your men who would even be close."

Albertson turned his attention back to what had just

happened. "Well, boys, none of what was said back there is to be discussed with anybody, you understand? I expect I will hear how Mrs. Canfield turns up missing. So I feel the best thing for us is to pull in our horns and let Wells Gorman handle the lady in his own fashion. It's his affair."

Mary Agnes watched Alvin Albertson and his two men ride off in the direction of the Pitchfork. "I'm glad you were here, Mr. Boone," she said.

"I'd like you to call me Travis, ma'am. That is, once you get to know me, if it's all right with you."

"That's what I'll do from this point forward . . . Travis."

Boone stepped into the saddle and rode around the corner of the porch, holding up when she motioned him to pause.

She gave him a long, sincere look. "Before you start your ride, I've changed my mind. I would like you to—"

"I was fixing to ask you. You want me to look around for your son? I'll do that. I need to take a look at those mountains, anyway. My family raised me in mountains like those."

"I'm sorry to bother you with—"

"I don't mind at all. That's why you hired me, ma'am."

"Well, I'm sure you understand my concern. Hoke should have been home last night. It's the first time he hasn't come back. I'm frightened he's gotten himself into trouble, and—"

"Where does he usually ride when he goes off like that?"

"Up around Eagle Pass, mostly. He has a friend who lives up on one of the ridges. You can see Eagle Pass from there. You can also see Creed's grave. You won't have any problem finding the pass. If Pete took the Wheatland road . . . you must've ridden within sight of the Licking River's South Fork. . . ."

Boone realized how difficult it was for her to ask him to

search the unknown countryside for her son the day after their very first meeting, but this would be as good a time as any to introduce himself to the youngster and maybe let him know he was still a young pup to his mother.

"I'll find him, ma'am," he said. "I've always enjoyed the mountains. Sorta gives me a feeling of being where I was born."

"Thank you," she said. Her voice quavered slightly.

Chapter Five

It was late in the afternoon when Boone rode past Eagle Pass. He reined the Appaloosa at the foot of a steep slope and dismounted near a growth of buffalo grass, among what at first appeared to be a dozen horse tracks and wagon-wheel pockmarks.

A quick wind swirled off the rocky hillside. After leading his horse no more than a hundred feet farther up the hillside, he found a single stick of dynamite caught in a patch of thorny brush where it had probably fallen from a wagon. On the far side of the brush he caught sight of an empty cardboard box with a label marked PITCHFORK in large, crude letters.

He placed the dynamite in a saddlebag and remounted, then rode on up the slope, where he found a young man—Hoke Canfield, he presumed—stretched out on the ground beneath a quilt, unconscious and looking like a soul close to death.

He also found a tall black man standing on the far side of a gray horse and wagon with a Remington resting across the horse's rump. The man had a fixed smile on his face.

"Hello," Boone said quickly.

The man nodded. "Howdy there," he replied. "I saw you looking around down there. You a lawman or something, mister?"

"Nope."

"Well, then, who *are* you?"

"I'm Travis Boone. Who're you?"

"Critter Malone. I'm a friend of the Canfields."

"Well, then, glad to meet you, Critter," Boone said as he dismounted. "Is that Mary Agnes' son, Hoke, there?"

"Yes, sir, it's him all right. You know Hoke?"

"Not personally, but I know his mother, and I've heard a lot about him. That's why I'm up here. His mother's been real concerned of his whereabouts. She wanted me to ride up here and take a look around for him."

"She had a job opening," Critter said. "You take that job?"

Boone nodded. "I took it for the winter. Looks like the boy's been shot up some."

Critter made a face and said, "He has a scratch on his gun arm. It's not much, but there's a worse one in his chest. It's gonna take some time to get well, but I figure him to make it."

"Looks bad."

"Bad enough, I reckon."

"You got any idea on who did the shooting?"

Critter shook his head. "Uh, no, not really, but I've seen a couple of gunmen riding with some of the Pitchfork bunch." Critter walked around the wagon and placed his rifle and Hoke's pistol and repeating rifle in the wagon bed.

Boone asked, "You think the men who shot him were from the Pitchfork?"

Critter stared at Boone for a moment. "I'd say they could be, but if they were, I got a feeling it was without the blessing of Wells Gorman. Right now Wells is doing all he can to be friendly with Mary Agnes. He'll probably hang the man who shot Hoke."

Boone thought for a moment, then looked to the sky, where two turkey buzzards flew over the rim of the ridge. At a greater distance, on a smaller south ridge, two more rose higher for the air currents.

"Looks like we're about to have company from up above," Boone said.

"Yeah. Looking for a dead cow, likely."

"What about the boy?" Boone said, nodding toward Hoke Canfield.

"Like I said, he'll be okay. He's a tough youngster, that boy."

It didn't take Critter long to check on Hoke before gently moving him to the wagon bed with a rolled-up ground blanket placed beneath his head. "I need to get him up to my cabin. If you want, you can follow me up there."

Boone followed.

The cabin was thirty or forty yards over the ridge rim and sitting in the midst of a group of thick-trunked pine and scattered buffalo brush. Winter wood was cut and stacked against the front wall of the cabin within easy reach.

With Hoke still unconscious, Critter carried him inside the cabin and placed him on an Army cot against the back wall with little effort. "He needs to rest the night," Critter said. "We'll leave at first light. It's a pretty good piece for him to be moved right now. Besides, I've got a feeling Mary Agnes isn't as worried as she was, now that she's got you out here, prowling around."

Boone grunted.

Critter smirked at him.

* * *

After a late-afternoon supper of Navy beans cooked in hog fat and a plate of fried corn bread, Critter took his rifle and walked out the front door to peer around. Boone was sitting at the table cleaning his gun when Critter returned and lit another kerosene lamp.

"I see you've caught yourself a habit," Critter told Travis, admiring the way Boone's hands moved about his handgun. "Most men with a reputation never forget how to clean their gun, it seems."

" 'Reputation'? What does that mean?"

"It means I know who you are, *Alex* Boone."

Boone leaned back in the chair. He picked up his gun and looked at the two carved letters on its stock: AB. He'd meant some time back to remove those initials but never got around to it.

"Most folks know me as Travis Boone."

"That's fine with me. You had quite a reputation back then, didn't you?"

"That's old news, Critter," Boone said. "I'd like to keep it that way, if we're going to stay friends."

"I don't mind, but gunfighting is seldom old news. I heard you went to busting horses. Just up and quit, folks say. To me that would be a hard thing to do—just up and quit, that is."

"Actually it was the safest thing I've done lately."

Critter chuckled. "I wouldn't let it worry me none, was I you. Right now you're gonna need all of what you've learned over the years. Wells Gorman is down there at his big old Pitchfork thinking about how you rode in here and sold your gun to Mary Agnes, and he'll be letting his men know what they're up against."

"That's too bad. But I didn't 'sell my gun.' "

"I know that, but let him think what he wants to think,

Mr. Boone," Critter said. "No need to let that man feel he's got life by the tail feathers."

Boone shrugged. "Speaking of Gorman," he said, "what's really on his ticket?"

"You haven't heard?"

"I've heard some things, of course, especially about the canal he wants dug over there, but that's about it. And how much he wants to hold the hand of Mrs. Canfield."

"Yes, sir. That's two things he'll never get."

Critter stepped away from the table and opened the cabin door again. He pointed downhill. "Right down there is Eagle Pass. I'm sure Gorman's not finished just yet, Mr. Boone, and he'll see you as another man standing in his way of gaining Mary Agnes' hand. When she strung up that Ellwood Spread barbwire across Eagle Pass, that told him he needed to come up with another plan."

"She seems to be a fine lady," Boone said. "Somebody needs to look out for her, from what it sounds like."

Critter nodded. "Well, from this end of things it appears to me she's found that man, Mr. Boone," Critter said. "Now, she's a smart woman, that lady. Nobody's gonna pull the wool over her eyes. And now she's got *Alex* Boone working for her, in my humble opinion, that's all she'll need to keep Gorman in his place."

"My name is Travis," Boone said abruptly. "Nobody calls me Alex."

Critter watched as Boone replaced each round into his Walker Colt with a little more force, using his thumb to shove each one into its place.

Critter smiled. Boone's way with guns was a good thing to remember, he thought. It would keep him ahead in the game.

Chapter Six

Wells Gorman was well versed in how to use his wealth and hired guns to his advantage. At this particular moment, though, he was staring intently at Tommy Kerns, expecting a lot more out of the young Texan than he was receiving. The skin on Gorman's large-boned face was drawn as tightly as a cinch on a Texas saddle.

"What th' hell you saying to me, kid?"

Kerns shrugged. "It's just what I been hearing," he said. "Maybe there's nothing to it."

He had just told Gorman how one of his men had shot Hoke Canfield, killed Turkey Adams, and left Hoke to die somewhere on a ridge across from Eagle Pass.

Gorman stalked to the far wall of his main room. He reached for an eight-foot bullwhip hanging on a spike, removed it, and turned to stare out the large window at the bunkhouse, where a man stood washing his arms and chest. Two Pitchfork regulars stood silently with their backs to a large stone fireplace, watching Gorman snap the whip across the floor as if popping a rattler's eyes.

40

Carter Sims, the Pitchfork foreman, stood with his left elbow on the fireplace mantel. Opposite him, with his arms crossed, was Ed Snowden, Gorman's most trusted employee. Snowden had been with the Pitchfork longer than any other rider.

Gorman turned from the window and glared at Kerns. "Who told you this?"

"That new man you hired last week," he said.

"What new man?"

"The one that rides that blue-eyed albino, the one that rode in here from Hays City claiming he was some kind of kin to Wes Hardin. Says he rode with Hardin on the Chisholm Trail up to Abilene when they were both young whippersnappers."

"Harlan Stiles said that?"

"Yes, sir, him and some of the boys, along with a bunch of Albertson's irrigation crew, rode up to take a look at Eagle Pass. While they were there, they tore down that string of barbwire Mary Agnes had put up across that gap. They was all set to punch a big hole in the South Fork with dynamite when Hoke and Turkey Adams started throwing lead at them from up on a nearby ridge."

Gorman's face turned blood red. "Damn it to hell, I told Albertson to stay off the Deuce until I got some things settled with Mary Agnes; *then* he was to start his digging. If I'm going to swing her around to my way of thinking and get that canal dug before the winter sets in, I sure as hell don't need somebody meddling where they're not invited to meddle. I explained to him we were dealing with a woman who thinks I had something to do with her husband's killing. What th' hell's she going to think now?"

"There's more," Kerns said. "Two of his men were hit."

"Was Albertson there?"

"I don't know. Stiles didn't say. But a couple of Albertson's men were there, and I'm sure Albertson has already heard who put a bullet into the Canfield boy and who killed Turkey Adams."

Kerns stood up and walked to the fireplace to share some of the warmth. He wanted to get through with this so he could return to the bunkhouse.

"Okay," Gorman growled. "It's over and done." He stared at Kerns. "You plan on telling me which one of my men shot Hoke, or am I going have to drag it out of you?"

Kerns shook his head. "The word I heard was McNabb."

"The Canfield boy's dead, then?"

Kerns shook his head. "No, sir, I didn't say he was dead. I said he was shot."

Gorman glared. "Anybody check on him to make sure?"

"I heard they wanted to," Kerns answered. "One of them started up the hill to check on him but was stopped in his tracks by a black man with a Remington. He rode up on them and started popping at them from high up on that hillside where he lives."

"Where'd he come from?"

"There's an old line shack up there. I heard he lives there. Probably hired by Mary Agnes a while back to keep an eye on Eagle Pass," Kerns said. "I've seen him and the Canfield boy riding around together looking for wild cows."

Sims grudgingly moved aside to allow Kerns to stand close enough to feel the fire's warmth, then walked to the door. Before he left the room, he paused just long enough to say, "Well, boss, I guess that about hog-ties her hands, don't it? As for those Nebraska ditch-diggers, I reckon they can start any day now."

"Not so damn fast," Gorman said. "We're not ready until I say we're ready. Everybody understand that?"

It was a known fact that Gorman had very little sympathy or none at all for any man who dared ignore one of his orders. He turned to stare at Sims, who was holding the door open for Snowden.

"You tell McNabb I'm coming to see him," Gorman said. "He'll wish to hell he had never set foot on the Deuce. When I'm finished with him, Sims, I want you and Stiles to get the horses ready. We're gonna ride up north and do some fence-mending."

"Fence-mending? Where?" Snowden asked.

"The Double Deuce, damn it."

Snowden stared at him. "You think that's a good idea . . . this soon?"

"Probably not, but we'll just say we're up there to pay our respects. I sure's hell don't need Mary Agnes thinking I gave the order to hurt that boy of hers. I need to get that settled, then I'll deal with Albertson. He needs to be told who the hell he's working for."

Sims and Snowden turned and walked out the door.

Gorman motioned for Kerns to take a seat, which he did. "All right, now, Tommy, after we're finished paying our respects to Mary Agnes, I want you to ride on down to the south pasture, find Albertson, and haul his ass up to the Pitchfork. I want him up here first thing tomorrow. That's an order."

"No problem," Kerns said. "What about the Deuce? You want me along?"

Gorman exhaled wearily. "Yeah, of course I do . . . this has turned into a nasty mess. I've been hearing Mary Agnes hired some gunslinger. That's another burr under my saddle. I'd like you with us in case he's trouble."

Kerns stood up to leave. "The word I have is, he's from Montana," he said.

"Montana?"

"Yes, sir, a former bronco peeler. Name's Travis Boone. They say he worked for old Bill Yates up there at the Rafter K for a long while. And that ain't all I heard. He had a reputation as some kind of tough gunman back in his younger days," Kerns explained.

Gorman's eyes narrowed. "Huh. Why would Mary Agnes hire a man like that?"

"Seems pretty clear to me. He's a gunfighter."

After a pause, Gorman said, "Okay, so he's a gunfighter. I still want you to check around. Find out who he really is, what he's up to, and what Mary Agnes has on her mind. If you think we're in for some trouble, I want to know—and I want to know ahead of time! This thing with her and Eagle Pass has to be settled before the weather turns on us."

"What about Albertson?" Kerns asked.

"What about him?"

"Did you send him to the Deuce?"

"Absolutely not."

"Well, he was there."

"What th' hell was he doing up there?"

"Way I heard, he was telling Mary Agnes why you needed a canal dug. She ran him off. Boone was there with her, watching the whole thing like he'd been paid to do," Kerns said.

"Albertson alone?"

"Nope. He brought them two henchmen of his, but they kept their mouths shut and their hands clear of their guns when they saw Boone, that's for sure."

"Where's Albertson's crew now?"

"Far's I know, they're still on the south pasture. It's sort of a tent camp they built down there."

His face expressionless, Gorman walked to the front window again and looked across the yard to the men's bunkhouse. "We'll talk later, kid. I've got some things to do before we head out."

He'd seen Solly McNabb washing his armpits at a water trough. He stalked out the front door, bullwhip in his hand. Kerns followed him as far as the front porch. He found a chair leaning against the outside wall and remained behind.

McNabb looked up. Gorman was striding toward him with stiff-backed hostility, the bullwhip firmly gripped in his right hand.

McNabb smiled at Gorman as Gorman approached and said in his most conversational tone, "Morning, boss, how're you doing?"

Gorman stopped abruptly, his feet set wide apart, the whip stretched out threateningly to one side. That should have been enough of a warning to McNabb, but he just stood with his big arms hanging loose at his sides, staring at Gorman with a foolish grin on his unshaven face.

"Who told you to shoot Hoke Canfield?"

"Nobody, boss."

"Do you plan on telling me why you shot him?"

"It was not like I intended to kill him. Actually it was just a wild shot, boss. I was trying to scare him off, that's all. Him and Turkey came up on us before we knew it. We was planning to set off a couple sticks of dynamite and scare the britches off both of them. But they went to shooting. Hit one of Albertson's men 'fore we knew what was going on. I shot back. Didn't aim at nothing. When they kept shooting, I got out of there. Nobody told me Canfield was shot dead."

"You didn't know you killed him, you're saying?"

"Yes, sir, that's what I'm saying."

"You're a stupid man, McNabb! You know that? All you've ever done around here is cause me trouble, and I'm fixing that right now! I want you saddled and fogging out of here before I bury you right where you stand. You understand?"

McNabb didn't answer.

He finished tucking the tail of his black shirt into his pants, and then he turned and faced Gorman, working nervously with the final button on his shirt. After buttoning it, he adjusted his gun belt and shrugged his meaty shoulders and said, "Well, now, Mr. Gorman, what you're saying to me ain't right at all. I've done you a big favor, and you oughta appreciate that."

Gorman glared at him. "Favor?"

"Yes, sir. Maybe now that widow woman will know you mean business. She's about finished! You just wait and see if I ain't right. I got it done for you. If nothing else, she'll sell that piece of land and get out of Wyoming on the first train to New Orleans."

McNabb was still smiling as eight feet of braided rawhide swept out across the yard.

"Watch it with that thing!" he yelped, grabbing at the braided line with his left hand and missing. He stumbled back several feet as Gorman moved in closer, his face raging red.

Gorman drew the whip back a few feet, and the rawhide stretched out with a loud popping sound, this time cutting a red line on McNabb's white belly, inches above his belt line. Blood showered from the long gash, and then another one. The big man clawed at the whip as it struck again, opening another ugly furrow across the bridge of his nose, wrapping snakelike around his neck before being jerked back for another flash of stinging rawhide that cut the left side of his chest.

"I'll kill you for that!" McNabb screamed.

Gorman snapped his arm and wrist once again, stepping easily aside, avoiding McNabb's rush and at the same time punishing him with the rawhide tip twice.

Sims yelled from the doorway. "For God's sake, boss, you've cut him up bad! He's gonna be blind."

Gorman changed hands with the whip. "I'm gonna blast him right through the gates of hell!" Gorman's gun hand came up and he shot McNabb twice. McNabb spun around and appeared ready to run, but his knees gave way and his big body crumpled to the ground, his hand sliding off his revolver butt.

Gorman spun around, screeching at Sims, "All right! You and Snowden bury that fat son of a dog where I won't smell him. When that's done, I want you saddled up and ready to ride. We're gonna take a ride up to the Deuce and pay Mary Agnes a visit."

Sims grunted. "She just lost her son, boss."

Gorman flared. "That's why we're going up there, you idiot. She needs some comforting, and I'm the man who needs to do it. Somebody's got to smooth this thing over before it gets totally out of hand."

Sims roped Gorman's white-faced mare and saddled it for him. He led the horse across the yard to where Gorman stood on the front porch, waiting patiently. Tommy Kerns, Ed Snowden, and the new man, Harlan Stiles, were saddled and ready to leave for the Double Deuce, five miles to the north, within sight of the Licking River's South Fork.

Sims looked briefly at his partner, Snowden. "This may be a mistake," he said.

Snowden shrugged, as though he knew what Sims was thinking and halfheartedly agreed.

Gorman led off, riding well in front of the others.

Chapter Seven

From the front porch, Mary Agnes watched the five men in yellow rain slicks ride out of the mist less than a quarter mile south. She kept them in her sight as they turned their horses for the Double Deuce ranch house.

She took a deep breath. She knew what was coming. She had been expecting them for several days now and wondered why they had picked such a lousy day to make their ride up there.

Hoke was sleeping. Travis and Critter Malone were seated at the dinner table having coffee and talking about how they needed to get some hay baled and ready before winter arrived.

Mary Agnes came in from the porch. "Pitchfork riders coming," she said. She returned to the porch with her shotgun.

Travis and Critter followed her out the door. "Which one's Gorman?" Boone asked.

"That's him on the white-face," Critter said. Positioned on Mary Agnes' right, Boone cradled his loaded Remington in his long arms. He walked to the opposite side of the porch and leaned back against the wall so he would be in the shadows of the low-hanging roof.

"Who're the others, ma'am?" he asked, looking over at Mary Agnes.

"There's Carter Sims, Gorman's foreman," she answered calmly. "That's Ed Snowden and Tommy Kerns on his right. Sims is the one to keep our eyes on. He's something of a little sneak. Not very good with a gun, though, I've heard. Snarls a lot, so it's difficult to read what's on his mind."

Boone asked, "What about the one on the albino?"

She squinted into the drizzle. "Oh, him? I don't recall ever seeing that one."

"Do you know him, Critter?" Boone asked.

"No, he's new to me. I'd remember that horse."

The five men were riding abreast as they approached, their yellow slicks shining in the drizzling rain. Wells Gorman was the first to reach the porch and rein up, the brim of his cattleman's Stetson drooping from the downpour. He ignored Critter and Boone deliberately, his cold eyes going directly to Mary Agnes.

"Why, good morning, Mary Agnes," Gorman volunteered.

She didn't answer.

"I must say you're looking more attractive every time I see you. Being a widow hasn't made you hard looking, like many widows I know. Of course, you've always been a fine-looking woman." Gorman made a move to dismount, stopping when he saw Mary Agnes shaking her head at him.

"You're not invited, Mr. Gorman," she said softly but coldly. "You need to stay where you are and ride out of here.

You're not here on my invitation . . . and if you're here to make another offer, you're wasting your time and mine. I've already put your man Albertson in his place."

Gorman removed his hat and shook water from it, then returned it lower on his brow, bending the brim slightly to allow the water to drain. Boone could tell Gorman was swearing under his breath, even while his eyes were holding Mary Agnes'.

"That's no way to act after we rode all the way up here in this rain to pay our respects," he said.

Mary Agnes stared at him. " 'Respects'? Is that why you brought your gunmen with you?"

The wealthy rancher looked around. "Being neighbors, we just wanted to say how sorry we were to hear about your son being killed in a gunfight, Mary Agnes. We didn't know about it until one of my men told me he'd heard from somebody up in Six Mile that Hoke had been shot by some rustler."

The longer Boone watched and listened, the more convinced he became that Gorman was cooking his own goose as far as Mary Agnes was concerned.

"Your man heard wrong, Mr. Gorman. My son's not dead."

Gorman looked honestly surprised. Boone watched his eyes wander over to Boone and then back across the porch to Critter. When Gorman glanced back to Mary Agnes, he looked concerned that she had not lowered the barrel of her shotgun. In fact, she had moved the barrel more to her left, now leveling it squarely on Gorman.

And in firing position.

From the look on his face, Gorman apparently had expected to be greeted by a teary-eyed mother with her head in her hands, alone and frightened. Instead, she faced him with a shotgun and two gunmen flanking her, both with rifles and the means to do him and his men plenty of harm.

"Now, boys," he said, "let's all keep a cool head here."

"Hoke is alive and well, Mr. Gorman," Mary Agnes said. "When he's ready, he'll let me know who shot him, and then we'll be talking to Sheriff Johnson or Deputy Judd."

"That's good to hear, Mary Agnes. Maybe while we're here I could look in on him. We'd all feel better knowing who it was that shot him."

"He has no reason to tell you anything," Mary Agnes said. "If he did, I would expect him to say it was one of your men who shot him."

Gorman became defensive. "Now, now, that's not at all fair, Mary Agnes. It was someone's terrible mistake. I know that, but the way I understand it, the boys rode up there and caught a pack of rustlers with a calf down, and before they knowed what they'd rode into, bullets were flying thick as a beehive.

"It's a wonder they all didn't get killed. Hoke was mighty fortunate, I'd say. Things have a way of getting out of hand with bullets flying around in all directions. Naturally we're full of regret about what happened. Sometimes good people have a run of bad luck. I guess that's what we have here. Just the other day I was telling my men there should be a way we could help you and the boy survive up here with winter coming."

"What kind of help would that be?" Mary Agnes asked.

"Well, let's say, we could take over the operation of the Double Deuce for you. Work it like a ranch should be worked. We could do that, you know, and do it without a lot of trouble. Of course that would mean we would need some of our herd moved up to your lower range, where they could have water. That way it would be a big help to both of us, you know, and maybe later we could get together on building that canal I been telling you about."

Boone looked around at Mary Agnes. She looked ready for a scrap.

"For the final time," she said, "that'll never happen, so get that through your thick skull."

"Now look, Mary Agnes, if you'd just listen to me one time in your life, I could help you, honestly. Everybody knows you're having trouble," Gorman said, while trying to hold his temper. "If you'd just be a little more reasonable, I could loan you a couple of my men."

Mary Agnes said, "For what, Mr. Gorman?"

"Well, from the looks of things, it's plain to be seen you could use a good foreman and some men to care for the place. That way you wouldn't have to hire some busted-up bronco peeler and a black man who has to live in a run-down line shack. What're you paying him? From here he looks like the sort of man who'd work for rooming and a few square meals."

Boone cleared his throat. Gorman turned to look at him, faking surprise. "You have something you want to say to me, cowboy?"

Boone nodded. "Yes, sir. I was just standing over here wondering who you have in mind as a good foreman for the Double Deuce."

Wells Gorman answered with a smile. "Oh, I'd say most any one of my men could handle that job without breaking a good sweat."

A wan smile touched Boone's face. "I assume you feel sure of that," he said, and he moved out of the porch shadows, his gray eyes taking in each man for several seconds before moving on to the next, his rifle at his side. "I'd like to see that man, Mr. Gorman. Would you point him out for me? I'd like to see what he looks like in case we meet again."

With a quick nod of his head, Gorman said evenly, "Why, of course." He paused to nod his head toward the man on the albino. "I'd like you to meet Mr. Harlan Stiles. Harlan came all the way from Hays City to give us a hand with some of the dirtier things we sometimes have to do. There's little doubt in my mind that Harlan would do a fine job. Any more questions?"

Boone said casually, "One more. How good is he with dynamite?"

Gorman frowned. "What's that mean?"

Boone reached behind his back and with his left hand held up the stick of dynamite he'd carried with him from the living room.

Gorman shifted his weight and adjusted his hat again, staring at the stick of dynamite. "What th'—"

"It's dynamite, Mr. Gorman. I found this at Eagle Pass, near the elbow of the South Fork. Some of your men were up there, it seems, getting ready to practice their skill with sticks like this one. They must have dropped it in their hurry to get out of Mr. Malone's shooting range," he said, pointing his rifle across the porch to where Critter stood with his own rifle cuddled in his huge arms.

Gorman glared at Boone. "You think that thing belongs to the Pitchfork?"

"I *know* it belongs to the Pitchfork," Boone said. "Your men left the box it came in."

"Well, you're wrong, cowboy. My men haven't been off the Pitchfork for more than a week."

At that moment, Boone saw the slight movement the

Hays City man was making and waited to see how far he planned to take it. Although he kept his eye on Gorman, Boone knew that Stiles had his right hand at his side beneath the rain slick and had eased the leather thong from his gun's hammer with his thumb and forefinger. He also knew that Stiles had gently moved his gun up and out of its holster, inch by inch, until he had the gun palmed and pressed against his right thigh. If the need came, he probably thought he had given himself an edge.

Boone knew better.

He held the stick of dynamite in his left hand, balanced in the palm where Harlan Stiles could plainly see it. Stiles stared at the dynamite stick. When Boone made a motion to toss the dynamite to Stiles, Stiles reached out to grasp the explosive, but Boone pulled it back. "Hand this over to your boss so he can read the brand on it."

Stiles flinched. He recovered and made a swipe with his hand in a wasted attempt to snare the stick of dynamite, frowning. He began to wrap the reins of his albino around the saddle horn so he would have his left hand free while still holding his pistol close to his right leg. "What th' hell you doing?" he growled, and he reached out with his left hand for the stick of dynamite. "Let me have it."

Boone instead tossed the dynamite toward Stiles, who leaned over in his saddle but was still too far away. The dynamite fell to the ground in front of the albino's left hoof, and, as Boone had intended, brushed the horse's ankle. The slight blow was a surprise to the small horse. Its head came up in a jerk, eyes rolling around roguishly, and with a lunge of its body it hurled Stiles from its back. As he fell, Stiles made a fruitless grab for the saddle horn, lost his gun, and rolled unceremoniously beneath the horse. He landed stiff-legged and flat on his back in the snow and mud and began frantically raking the ground for his gun.

There were a series of grunts from Gorman and the others and a flurry of heel kicking and rein yanking as each man struggled to get the animals clear of one another—and the dynamite—just in case.

The menacing click of the gun in Stiles' right hand brought a yell from Gorman. "Stiles! Wait! Hold it!"

Mary Agnes saw Harlan Stiles' muddy face, his anger, and then the movement of his gun hand as he raised it off the ground. She didn't see Boone making his own move until she heard the single rifle shot and felt the blast of heat rush all the way across the porch.

Stiles grunted. The bullet caught his flashy Mexican belt buckle and ricocheted off to his right, boring a bloody red hole between the knuckle of his trigger finger and thumb.

The second shot from Boone's rifle busted Stiles' left knee. He let out a bloodcurdling scream and squirmed deeper beneath the albino's belly. The horse wouldn't stand still. Both front hoofs smashed into Stiles' shoulder.

"Damn you! You didn't need to shoot him," Gorman yelled.

Boone could hear Gorman's lungs sucking in air.

Carter Sims and Ed Snowden were still struggling to steady their horses, finally getting both under their control several feet from the porch, with their hands well clear of their holstered guns.

Gorman was still screaming and puffing. "We're not done here! It's not over! Nobody makes a fool of Wells Gorman!" He pointed a finger at Boone. "Your time will come—just you wait!"

Boone said, "I will."

Tommy Kerns took up his reins and moved his horse around Sims and over to where Boone stood on the edge of the porch, and leaning forward so he could look Boone in the eye, said, "You sure surprised Stiles there, Mr. Boone."

"It was his call."

"I don't know about that, but I thought I would let you know, a trick like the one you pulled on Stiles wouldn't have worked on Snowden or me. Stiles ain't all that bright."

Gorman twisted around in his saddle. "You heard what I said, cowboy: It's not over by a long shot. Your day will come. There'll be another time."

Kerns let his smile spread. "Good luck to you."

Boone stepped off the porch and picked up the dynamite and Stiles' pistol. He kept the pistol, stuffing it behind his belt. He handed the dynamite to Ed Snowden, who took it and with caution slid it very lightly into his saddlebag.

"I'll keep this handy," Snowden said. "We might need it to blow up a stump or two. If Stiles wants his gun, what's he to do about it?"

"It's his gun," Boone said. "He can come by for it on his way back to Hays City. If he doesn't want it, I'll keep it, so I can remember how close I came to killing him."

Sims and Snowden stepped down from their horses to help drag Stiles out from beneath the albino and into his saddle.

Gorman turned angrily to Snowden. "When we get back, you pay Stiles what he has coming, Ed, and get rid of him. I thought he could handle a little trick like that in his sleep."

"I don't think—"

"Get him out of my sight!"

Snowden shrugged and told Stiles to keep his mouth shut and to keep on riding.

Mary Agnes waited until they were out of sight before she walked over to Boone. She smiled sweetly and said, "Well, I'll be dogged, as my husband always said. I think I'd better keep an eye on you, Travis."

Chapter Eight

That night, after she finished peeling and cutting potatoes into small chunks for potato soup, Mary Agnes heated an extra pan of water to tend to her son's wounds. Hoke had been tossing and turning for more than an hour. His arm wound was just a scratch, but the one in his chest had opened slightly and was showing some dampness through the bandage she had placed on him earlier, when Boone and Critter first brought him home in a wagon.

"I need to tend to Hoke," she said, leaving the soup boiling on the stove. "He looks peaked."

"He any better?" Boone asked.

"Some."

Critter and Boone followed her from the front room into Hoke's bedroom and stood back while she lightly bathed the ugly chest wound, changing the damp bandages twice before getting him to settle down and allow her to cover it with roasted prickly-pear leaves to remove any inflammation.

Critter and Boone had returned to the front room and were seated at the table with a cup of coffee in their hands when Mary Agnes returned with a bowl of potato soup for each man. But Boone was not hungry. He had barely spoken a word since the incident with Gorman's men. In his younger days, when he was twenty, he would have gone on as if nothing had happened worth talking about, but those times were long gone. He had shot a man today because he didn't like his stance, and now he was wondering how that sat with Mary Agnes. Did she resent having to watch a man get shot? Would she blame him for the way he'd gone about it? Did she think the shooting was unnecessary? Would she even bring it up? He wasn't sure what he would say to her.

When Mary Agnes returned to her son's bedroom, Critter looked across the table at Boone, frowning and shaking his head. "What's wrong with you?"

Boone told him how he felt.

"Well, I never heard such," Critter exclaimed. "If she has anything she wanted to say to you about what happened out there, you'd have already heard it. Besides, you could've killed him, and you didn't. She respects that."

Boone looked down at the gun in his holster and said, "Maybe that's a good place for it—holstered."

"You don't know a lot about women, do you?" Critter said, as though he had his mind made up.

Boone answered Critter cautiously. "Does anybody?"

"Well, I know this much. You keep going like you are, and you'll wind up too blame old and senile to care one way or the other," Critter said.

Boone stared at him and then smiled, but glumly. "I—all right, you're probably right."

Critter smiled. "You're the worst I've ever seen. That lady thinks a whole lot of you, Travis. I've noticed the way she looks at you. And I'm not talking about puppy love—that lady admires you. I haven't seen her look at a man like that for a long time."

Suddenly Boone felt foolish.

When Mary Agnes returned and took her seat at the table, Boone got up and warmed her coffee from a pot on the stove and said, "Looks like Hoke is going to be just fine, ma'am. He's from good stock, you know. All he needs is a few more days on that big feather bed."

"Why, thank you for that, Travis," she said. "He's really fortunate to have you and Critter as his friends, and that goes for me also."

Critter smiled broadly.

Boone sipped his coffee.

The following morning during breakfast, Boone told Mary Agnes that he planned to ride up to Six Mile Junction so he could explain to Deputy Pete Judd what had actually happened at the Double Deuce.

But Mary Agnes wasn't sure that telling Pete all the facts would make any difference. The law was the law, and a man had been shot. "You think that's necessary?" she asked.

"To me, it is."

She dropped a spoonful of sugar into her coffee. "Well, I guess you know best."

"While I'm there," Boone said, "I'll find a couple of men to help bring the herd down here."

"You could wait for Hoke to get better, Travis. I don't think Mr. Hays would mind holding the herd for a few more weeks. And as far as what happened recently, Pete may already know."

"It's better I do the talking to Pete, ma'am," Boone said. "And it will take more than a few weeks for Hoke to be well enough to deal with a bunch of stubborn cows. Besides, I'm going to be in Six Mile, anyway. I might as well start earning my bed and chuck. There's a good chance of bad weather coming, so we might be a little late getting the herd moving this way."

Mary Agnes could tell that Travis had made up his mind and didn't want it changed. "If that's what you think needs to be done, I'm good with it, but I would like you to do me one more favor."

"Of course. Name it."

"I'd like you to stop by Tate Parker's place. You'll be passing by there if you take the Wheatland road. It's on the right, just past a large pond."

"What'll I find there, ma'am?"

"Tate's got two boys—Josh and Jason. They're good with cattle. They've helped us before when the barn needed repairing and when things around our place needed fixing, and with moving our stock to the south pasture, when we had stock. I'm sure they'd be willing to give you a hand."

"I'll do that."

"Good. I appreciate it. If you would, just tell Mr. Parker I need their help. These are boys you can trust to do the job."

Boone chuckled to himself as he rode off. That was a shrewd woman. Having the Parker boys riding along was like hiring a cook's aide to watch the cook.

Chapter Nine

Tate Parker's house was set back a quarter mile from the rutted stage road. Boone barely remembered its being there when he rode by with Pete Judd, but he'd had other things on his mind.

He turned the Appaloosa toward the house. As he closed in, he could see a strong-looking, sprawling wood structure and a large barn with a pole corral a few feet away. Boone studied the rawboned old man standing in the yard. He stood with his hand on the butt of the old Frontier Colt stuffed in the waistband of his baggy corduroys. Behind him, a tall woman with some heft to her shoulders and hips appeared at the door of the house. She held a double-barreled shotgun, hammers under her thumb.

Always a shotgun, it seemed.

Boone touched the brim of his hat. "Tate Parker?" he asked, remaining in the saddle, his hands in plain sight.

The man nodded. "I'm Tate. Who're you?"

"Travis Alexander Boone."

"You from around here, Mr. Boone?"

63

"No, sir."

"You didn't say where."

"I'm from a lot of places, Mr. Parker. Montana mostly. Right now I'm from the Double Deuce. I'll be spending the winter there, taking care of some things that need taking care of."

"Mary Agnes send you to me?"

"Yes, sir, she asked me if I'd stop by on my way to Six Mile Junction. She said you might be able to give me some help moving a few cattle she bought from a man called Hays up there in Six Mile."

"I didn't know she'd bought any cattle." Parker studied Boone for a while and then said, "I reckon you're that feller who shot that Hays City gunman Wells Gorman hired."

"We had a misunderstanding."

"He should've known better."

"Stuff like that sure gets around fast down here."

"It does. We're glad to hear Mary Agnes has someone to help her git through the winter. Maybe things have changed for a spell at the Deuce. Ma and me always told Mary Agnes that one of these days she was gonna need to find herself a man who had the sand to buck those sorry Pitchfork dogs. They've been barking and snapping at that nice lady ever since her husband was ambushed and killed. It's about time someone took 'em to the woodshed."

Boone dismounted and let the reins fall to the ground. The woman in the doorway continued to eye him with caution before moving from the doorway and returning with two rangy, clean-faced young boys. Both had straw-colored hair and healthy faces. They walked past her and on across the yard to face Boone, nodding.

"Howdy." Boone met the two look-alike brothers with a

steady gaze. He accepted the handshakes they offered him, aware of the way they wore their guns, slightly low and without hammer thongs, one on the left and the other on the right hip.

"These are my boys," Tate Parker said. "Josh an' Jason. That suspicious-looking woman there giving you the keen eye is my wife, Sudie Mae. We're from the Blue Ridge Mountains. Took to living here some five years back. Liked it well enough to stay."

Boone nodded at Sudie Mae. His gaze went to her sons. "How can you tell which is which, ma'am? They look like twins."

"Oh, they're twins all right, Mr. Boone, but there's a whole lot of difference 'tween 'em. Jason there's left-handed and kinda surly when things ain't goin' his way. Josh is one of them other kind. He likes to talk and eat."

She lowered the shotgun for the first time and set it inside the door. "Well, here's hoping you take on that job of hers for good, Mr. Boone. You could at least spend more than the winter. Mary Agnes sure enough needs some good help. Should you need any from my family, you can count on us. Soon as the boys git done with some chores that need finishing, I'll send them on their way to Six Mile. You won't need more'n them two to handle those cows of hers. That is, if they's all a-sittin'."

Boone nodded. "I appreciate this very much."

"It's my pleasure," the old man said, "but there is one thing I want you to do, Mr. Boone."

"You name it, sir."

"If there's any trouble along the way and either one of our boys gets a bullet in him while he's riding with you . . . I'd like you to do me a favor, Mr. Boone."

"I'll do that.

"You kill the man what put it there."

Boone took the long way to Six Mile Junction by leaving the Wheatland stage road and cutting across the southern section of the Double Deuce range, mainly so he could have a look at Eagle Pass in case Albertson had decided to send some of his men over there, regardless of being warned to stay off Deuce land.

Everything seemed quiet enough.

From a distance he spotted the barbwire stretched across the gap between the two ridges. Someone had restrung it—he assumed Critter Malone.

An hour later, he took a turn around Six Mile Junction, looking for the cattle pen, and spotted the Parker twins. Surprised to see them sitting their horses in front of Hays' holding pen on the far side of a livery barn, he rode up and asked, "How'd you get here so fast?"

"We took the old Cheyenne warrior trail. It's shorter by a mile or so," Josh said.

Nodding and smiling, Jason pointed at the milling cattle. "They're good-looking animals. Polled Angus. We looked 'em over and didn't see an acorn in the whole bunch. Pa always said Morgan took better care of his business than anybody around."

A thin, slightly stooped man with long, rusty sideburns and a rust-colored mustache strolled from the south end of the stock pens. "I'm Lars Jessup. You fellers must be from the Double Deuce," he said.

"We are," Boone answered, and he told the man his name. "They're already paid for, right?"

"They are. About a hundred head, ear-marked and

shallow-forked." Jessup paused when he saw Boone watching a rider move around the far corner of the holding pen and turn his horse in their direction. "That's a Pitchfork rider," he said. "Ed Snowden. Ed's been up here most of the day looking to make a deal for the Deuce cattle, but Mr. Hays turned him down flat. He'd made his deal with Mary Agnes, and that's the way it was to stand. You know him?"

"We've met," Boone said.

Snowden nodded to Boone as he reined his mount. "Looks like Mary Agnes has a good bunch of young cows back there, Mr. Boone," Snowden said. "I figured I'd wait around so we could do some talking. I was up here looking for some cattle myself, but they're all bought and paid for, it seems."

Boone met his stare. "What's there to talk about?"

Snowden frowned. "Oh, uh—" he started; then he lowered his eyes to Boone's hand resting on his Walker Colt. "Well, uh, you've been with the Double Deuce long enough to know there's a small problem between your boss and my boss."

"I've felt that at times."

"Well, it's like this. Mr. Gorman needs water to finish one of his projects, but to get that water he has to have a canal dug so he can tap into the South Fork. Of course, that's on the Deuce land, and Mary Agnes won't—"

"I know all about the canal," Boone said.

"Yeah, you probably do, but have you heard our side?"

"Don't need to. Your boss doesn't have a side I'm interested in, Mr. Snowden," Boone interrupted. "The South Fork is out of bounds for the Pitchfork, and he knows it. There's no chance he'll dig a canal."

"The man needs more water. He's been hauling from some of his streams and pouring it into the reservoir from miles off, but it won't be enough to feed the lines he had planned."

"He should've thought about that before he made his plans," Boone suggested.

Snowden gazed at Boone. "Makes no sense to deny him access to the South Fork. In my way of thinking, it would be a good thing for both of them. Besides, I think one of these days they'll likely get hitched."

Boone said, "Who knows what makes sense these days? I recognize Gorman's water and conjugal problems, but since somebody put a bullet into Hoke, there's no chance you'll see any change this century. As far as getting hitched . . . that'll never happen."

"What are you saying?"

"I'm just saying, as it now stands, when Gorman sinks a spade into Eagle Pass dirt or we find another stick of dynamite anywhere near there, that'll be the day he will hate the very thought of digging a canal."

Snowden frowned at Boone and said, "Now, wait just a minute, Boone. I . . . uh . . . Wells had nothing to do with that woman's son getting shot, or anything Albertson's men did, if that's what you're thinking."

Boone was beginning to wonder how long it would take before Snowden lost his patience. He'd already lost his. He leaned forward in the saddle and said, "I've heard enough about Wells Gorman."

Snowden stared at Boone's Walker Colt and the fast-draw holster again. Boone knew there were only one or two things Snowden could do if he planned to stand his ground. He wondered which one it would be just as Snowden chose to go for his gun.

Boone had no intention of getting into a gun battle in

Pete Judd's backyard, yet he couldn't stand idly by while being threatened by some angry Pitchfork rider who thought himself a matchmaker. With both boot heels jabbing into the soft belly of his Appaloosa, Boone sent the big animal straight into Snowden's mare with such force that Snowden was thrown bodily from his saddle, landing hard on the back of his neck.

Boone came off the Appaloosa without a waste of motion and was standing over the Pitchfork gunman before Snowden knew what had happened. Snowden, his face distorted with rage, twisted out from beneath Boone and tried to stagger to his feet, but he was hit twice in his mouth by Boone's right and left fists. A sudden grunt of pain brought a half-strangled cry from Snowden, who was on the ground, crawling on his knees with a broken nose, searching wildly for his revolver.

Boone reached out and grabbed him by his hair, jerking his head forward and smashing his face with the butt end of his Walker Colt. Snowden went to his knees again, this time dazed. Boone stood over him with his gun barrel shoved hard against Snowden's mouth, chipping one of his front teeth.

"Look at me, Snowden!"

"Wha—"

"I said, *look* at me."

Snowden stared and remained in a squatting position, his face bleeding in three different places. Boone reached a hand out and pulled him to his feet. "You go back to the Pitchfork, and you tell your boss I didn't start this fight, but now that he's opened the gate, I promise him I'll be the one who closes it. You got that?"

Snowden swayed on his feet, as he turned wordlessly

from Boone and struggled to get his left foot into a stirrup while clinging to the saddle horn with both hands. His strength had obviously deserted him. Boone nodded to Josh and Jason, and the twins dismounted and rushed over to help settle Snowden into his saddle. Josh shoved Snowden's gun into his holster. He looked at Snowden and, shaking his head, said, "I swear, Mr. Boone could've killed you. You've taken your last lucky turn. So why don't you just ride on out of here? It's all over with."

"That sounds like good advice to me." The voice came from a group of men who had gathered around the holding pen out of curiosity. Deputy Pete Judd stood holding his Winchester repeating rifle with a sour look on his face. "Do as Josh says, Ed—be on your way out of town. I told Sheriff Johnson that when he returned, he wouldn't find any dead men lying around. I don't wish to make a liar out of myself."

Snowden was barely able to remain in the saddle. He gripped the saddle horn with both hands to keep steady. He glared down at the deputy and said, "I'm finished here, Pete, so don't put your spurs in me." With those final words, he rode off, shoulders drooping, a beaten man.

Boone holstered his gun. "That thing at the Deuce was fair and square, Pete. I wanted you to hear it from me. That feller they brought with them—Harlan Stiles—he was itching to fight."

"I heard as much, and I figured there had to be a reason for you to shoot a man on the Deuce, in front of Mary Agnes," the deputy said indifferently, turning his head to the Parker twins, who were standing by their horses.

"I take it you two fellers will be riding with Travis when he moves this bunch of bovines, is that right?"

"Is there a problem, Pete?" Boone asked. "We can—"

"No—no problem, Travis, none at all. I just thought you might take some of your frustration out on these poor heifers, and figured I'd better warn the boys of your nature's other side."

Boone saw a little glint reach Pete's eyes as the group rode off toward Jessup, who held the holding-pen gate open and was standing out of the way of the stirring cattle.

"You fellers ride peacefully," Jessup said. "If that's possible."

Chapter Ten

Later that afternoon, when Ed Snowden rode around Eagle Pass to the Pitchfork's northern range, Wells Gorman and Carter Sims were camped there and waiting for Snowden to tell them how things had gone in Six Mile Junction between him and Travis Boone.

"Was Boone there?" Gorman asked.

"He was. So were the Parker boys."

"Yeah, well, you sure don't look like you got anything done up there, Ed," Gorman said gruffly. "Did you tell Boone we would pay him a hell of a lot more than he'd ever make at the Double Deuce?"

"No, sir, I didn't get the chance," Snowden answered plainly.

Gorman swore. "Yeah, well, I can see that. Looks like he come damn near to skinning you alive."

"He could have, I was told."

"So Kerns is right about him. Travis Boone's a gunfighter."

"He's more than that, sir."

"What else?"

"He's the kind of man what don't budge when you push on him, and you're making a mistake if you take him for granted."

"We'll see about that."

"You can if you want, but I'm not going against him. If it comes to a gunfight, you'll have to find someone else to do your shooting."

Gorman shrugged his meaty shoulders. "I had that already figured, Ed."

"Glad you understand. You want me to ride along with you to see Albertson?"

"No."

"What am I to do while you and Carter are away?"

"You can pack up."

"Pack up? For what?"

"You're fired."

Gorman motioned for Carter Sims to follow him and rode off down the grassy slope at an easy pace toward Alvin Albertson's Irrigations Unlimited tent camp, leaving Snowden staring bewilderedly.

They were not riding long before they came within sight of the camp. A flurry of pistol and rifle shots brought them to a dead stop on a half-mile rise of grassy land. They were able to see three wagons. No riders were in sight, except the four riders in the distance, riding hard south.

"Where'd those shots come from?" Gorman asked Sims.

"Looks like it was from Albertson's wagon. I think that's him squatting there on the left."

Actually, Gorman was more interested in the four riders he'd spotted on their way south. Hurrying cautiously off the rise, Gorman and Sims found Alvin Albertson sitting on the ground with his rifle beside his right leg and his back slumped against the wooden spokes of the wagon's front wheel. He was in bad shape. He had taken at least four shots from somebody's rifle and was without any hope of making it through the rest of the day.

A larger wagon, directly behind the one where Albertson sat, was full of folded tents and pieces of heavy trench-digging equipment. Whoever did all the shooting wasn't interested in the machinery, obviously.

A few feet away, a man lay sprawled across the third wagon's high-backed seat. He was dead, shot once in the face.

"There's another one in the wagon, boss," Sims said.

Gorman looked away from Albertson. "Looks like they had a one-sided war here," Gorman observed. He rode up closer, with Sims following him, before stopping a horse-length back, looking over the scene in mild shock. They found three other bodies, each with a gunshot wound to the head, some with their guns still holstered.

Gorman swung his horse around and rode over so he could look down on Albertson without having to change position in his saddle. "Looks like you've had more trouble here than you could handle, Mr. Albertson. You've 'bout reached the end of your bartering days in Wyoming."

Albertson blurted, "They shot me . . . stole my cash box and my horses . . . shot my men!"

Gorman remained in the saddle, a so-what look on his face. "It does appear that way," he said. "Who did it? Your own men?"

Albertson nodded emotionally. "Four of my . . . uh . . ."

"I'll swear," Sims said, leaning forward and looking at the holes in Albertson's chest. "Your own men? They sure did a job on you." He turned to Gorman. "Those are some mighty serious-looking holes there in his chest. . . . He hit anyplace else?" Sims asked. He wondered how many shots had caused the mass of blood on the front of Albertson's white businessman's shirt.

Gorman shrugged and stared down at the wounded man. "I guess this means you and me are no longer doing business with each other, Mr. Albertson. That reminds me . . . I've always said, if you want something done right, you got to do it yourself."

Albertson flared. "I'm not dead yet."

"I wouldn't bet on that. You're mighty close, far's I can tell."

"I need a doctor."

"A doctor? Hell's bells, you're in need of a doctor, all right, but I'm not sure we have time for that. You've lost a lot of blood, and we need to get this mess off my land. Those ugly-looking holes in your chest look bad enough to kill a plow horse. I'd say it's about over for you."

Gorman turned to Carter Sims and swung his horse around. "When he ain't looking, finish him off, and let's ride outta here."

Chapter Eleven

Mary Agnes heard the sound of horses moving about in the yard and roused Hoke from his sleep. He flung back his quilt and slid across the floor to peer out the window just in time to glimpse two wraithlike shapes moving around in the darkness within a few feet of the porch.

"Be careful," she said. "You're not as well as you think."

Hoke put on his boots. "Maybe not, but I can use the rifle to send them back to the Pitchfork. Get it for me."

Before she found the rifle, Mary Agnes heard a man shout, "Canfield! We know you're in there! Now, you listen to what we tell you, and listen good, you hear me? Don't go doing any shooting. We ain't here to do you no harm. We're here just to talk. Then we'll ride off without firing a shot."

Hoke yelled out, "You'll ride out now or take some lead."

Another man yelled from the dark, safely across the yard. "Wells Gorman wants both you and your red-haired momma clean out of Wyoming. You hear that, boy?"

Mary Agnes, standing in the bedroom doorway, asked, "What did he say, Hoke?"

"Nothing important, Mom." Dropping down to one knee at the window, Hoke rested his elbows on the window's lower frame, eased the hammer back on the rifle, and waited. Then, seeing movement in the shadows, he foolishly pulled the trigger.

A man yelled. "Watch it! He damn near hit my mustang!"

"Wells said he might not listen to reason."

"If that's the way it's gonna be, we'll drag both of 'em out of there feet first!"

Hoke looked at his mother for advice, holding fire this time. "Where's Critter? Did he leave?"

"No, I don't think so. He's probably asleep in the barn."

Minutes dragged past. Hoke waited. He was breathing with difficulty. Mary Agnes heard him and knew he should be in bed resting, but she also knew he wanted to be like his father and stand and fight to the last shot.

"Don't argue with them," she said.

"They've threatened us, Mom," he said, still having trouble breathing. "They're on our land!"

"That's all they're doing, is threatening."

Outside, a man hunkered low at the far end of the porch, and another man's shadow moved about on the opposite end of it. The sudden, sharp crack of a rifle came from the barn, sending porch splinters flying mere inches from the man's boot heels. Then another followed. This clipped the man in the knee and sent him tumbling off the porch, yelping and hobbling for his horse. Another man close by spun his animal around hard and collided with a man loping out of the moonlight. The blow from the horse sent the man sprawling. A third shot brought the man off the ground, grabbing wildly for his startled horse, cursing the rider who had knocked him off his feet.

"Look out! Somebody's in the barn!"

"It's that black man!"

Another two rifle shots and the three men were mounted and beating a furious path out of the yard, all bent over and belly-raking their spurs.

Hoke was up with his rifle raised in salute. Critter Malone stood just outside the barn door, returning Hoke's wave with his own rifle held high over his head. Mary Agnes had taken Critter his supper before dark and tried to talk him into spending the night in the house or the bunkhouse, but he preferred sleeping in the barn with the animals.

Afterward, making certain the wound in Hoke's chest was okay, Mary Agnes took the rifle to her bedroom and placed it near the head of the bed. She turned and walked back to the living room and looked around at the porch, a worried frown on her face.

She stood there for a few minutes gazing off into the distance. Finally she realized she was looking for Travis Boone and the Parker twins. It was hours before daybreak. They were probably bedded down for the night.

"I'm not worried," she said aloud. Which was not even close to the truth.

Boone and the Parker twins pushed the herd about twelve miles east along the flatland after leaving Six Mile Junction before Boone decided to bed them along the foothills of Red Clay Butte and start out fresh the next day. Although not exactly a premium place to camp, the grass, short as it was, would at least give the cattle a chance to mill around after being penned for a few days.

Josh thought they could continue to move the cattle once they were rested. "We could make our way after a bit without much of a problem," he said. "We've got a big moon over us, and most of what's ahead is flatland same as this, not counting that hump of land there. There's very little scrub brush along the way."

"No need to hurry," Boone suggested, dismounting. He wrapped the reins of the Appaloosa around the trunk of a small tree and unrolled his ground blanket.

"I was just thinking how Mary Agnes gets all panicky and starts worrying when things don't happen right off," Josh said. "She's been that way since we first knowed her. I don't think she'll ever change much."

Their progress had been uninterrupted during the early part of the drive from Six Mile, but not without some wandering by Jason and Josh, who were constantly riding out on the flanks of the herd like two busy sheepdogs, moving from land swell to land swell, threading the sparse stands of scrub brush and constantly checking their back trail. Twice they saw the flicker of lights far off.

"Case of nerves, I reckon," Josh said, when Jason rode up beside him.

Ever since the encounter at Six Mile Junction with Ed Snowden, they'd been in a state of apprehension. Ambush came to mind. It could happen anytime, anywhere along the way to Broken Hand Wells.

"We'll have no trouble moving the herd," Jason said, looking at Boone. "There's plenty of moonlight, if that's what you want to do."

"How about something to eat?" Josh asked.

Jason stood up. "I'll get something going. Once we reach the Wells, we'll be on our way home. Right now I could stand some salt bacon. How about you, Mr. Boone?"

"I'm fine," Travis said.

Jason got busy building a fire and then moved out of the billowing smoke to the opposite side of the fire. He was reaching for the skillet when the crack of rifle fire sang out of the night, followed by a flurry of pistol shots, each one thudding into the fire and ground. Not one shot was close, but Travis spun around and dove out of the fire's orange light, falling onto his stomach and rolling, as two bullets splattered the ground near his feet.

"Where'd they come from?" Jason shouted.

"Don't matter, brother, they're here now!" Josh replied.

Both Jason and Josh had somehow made it to their saddles for their rifles without taking any bullets and were lying on the ground sending blind, angry shots into the shadows of a small hillside above them.

Amazingly, their shots were effective enough to cause several shadowy figures to leap up and scramble for safety higher on the hillside. They could only assume the shooters were rustlers or Gorman's Pitchfork men.

Boone stared into the darkness, waiting, his gun in hand. He took a deep breath as he spotted two dark shapes in his rifle sight, standing straight up with their rifles resting on a large, round rock halfway up the hillside. He fired into the shadowy shapes and heard a man grunt, then watched him stand up, straight-backed, and topple over onto his left side to lay where he fell, unmoving. A bullet from higher up burned a straight line across Boone's left shoulder. A second bullet buried itself in the ground beyond the fire.

Somewhere in the distance, they heard cattle being put on the move. "They're after the cattle," Josh said. "What happened to our horses?"

"They're gone!"

"I thought they were tethered."

"They were."

The fire took another hit, sparks and ash scattering in all directions. Two horsemen swept around the hillside and raced past them, riding Indian fashion and firing wildly as they went hell-for-leather. A straggler didn't make it. Hit, he flung his rifle aside and pitched to the ground.

Josh yelled out, "You okay, Jason?"

"I'm fine!"

"Pitchfork riders?"

"Can't tell."

Travis was hunkered down on his knees when he knocked a rider higher up on the hillside out of his saddle. The man's horse, a small Indian pony, raced on. Another man and horse followed, moving fast, the man twisting in the saddle and cultivating the ground with pistol fire but with little success. Hoarse and angry shouts broke from the hillside as Boone peppered the area briefly. Two riders broke off the hillside in opposite directions, one having more trouble than he could handle when his horse skidded abruptly, head down, sending the rider head over heels into the thorny brush his horse had been trying to avoid.

"They're on the run!" Josh yelled.

Travis was on his feet with Jason right behind him, both aiming and raking the hillside brush with one shot after another. Suddenly a rider came out of the shadows and raced straight for Boone. Jason, nursing a crease across his shoulder, was looking the other way. Josh, frightened that Jason had been hit, yelled and fired without aiming, missing the rider who was hanging Indian style from the side of a dorsal-stripe dun but getting close enough to turn him away.

Boone moved quickly, leaping directly into the path of the streaking horse as it struggled for solid footing on the rocky hillside. The rider, seeing Boone with his rifle jammed to his shoulder, jerked on the reins hard, leaning to the left, but not quickly enough to escape Boone's rifle bullet from entering the animal's forehead.

Boone felt queasy after his bullet took the horse from under the man, but there had been no other way to slow the man and his horse's charge. He'd had no clear shot at the small man leaning over his saddle with both hands clinging to the horn. The front legs of the horse buckled, sending its rider spilling from the saddle and then falling on him, pinning him to the ground.

Jason yelled. "He's done for!"

"You know him?"

"Nope."

Boone had watched another rider flip through the air and then hit the ground directly in front of the dun, saw him roll over and scramble to his feet, only to be trampled by the horse's flailing hoofs. He now lay beside the dun. Both men were dead or at least knocked senseless.

Not long after, the remaining shooters gave up the attack and scattered out of rifle range, almost without a sound.

Travis looked around at the battered coffeepot and the skillet embedded in the ashes of their dying campfire.

"Well, all I can say is they picked a good place," he said.

Josh returned from up on the hillside, where he'd found a dead man. Travis holstered his gun and turned to Josh. "You hit?"

"Just a scratch. Nothing to worry about."

"Okay. Let's get on with it," Jason said.

Their horses were nearby, searching for blades of grass. Once they were mounted, Josh said, "Whoever they were, they'll keep after the herd all the way to Broken Hand

Wells; then I look for them to cut for Salt Creek. If I'm right, we could lose every blame cow Mary Agnes spent her money on."

"I don't think they were herd-cutters," Jason said. "It's like they were after our hides more than they were the cattle."

Boone rode over. "How far is it to the Wells?"

"Couple hours. If that old moon up there stays with us, we'll be fine."

A mile off, they picked up some roughed-up tracks. The rustlers had kept the cattle they'd gotten bunched up. "Looks to be only two men left," Boone stated.

Twice they reined up to listen, hearing nothing but the chirps of nervous crickets and the squeak of their own saddle leather.

"Won't be long now," Josh said. "My mare can smell the Wells."

Although Broken Hand Wells was unfamiliar to Boone, who knew very little of the Wyoming territory, the Parker boys knew it, having worked with men who planned their drives according to the availability of water. They arrived sooner than expected and made camp.

No one slept. They sat around drinking coffee and sighing.

At first light they left the camp, riding spread out, surveying the ground they'd just left but finding no sign of riders or herd having been anywhere near the Wells.

Shaking his head in disbelief, Josh said, "Something's peculiar about this."

Jason said, "You think they intended to drive the herd to the Pitchfork? Not me. I look for them to head straight for some canyon."

Josh and Jason exchanged glances. "That's it! They turned the herd before the cattle caught the scent of water."

"Why would they do that?" Boone asked. "They should have made for the water."

Jason exclaimed, "Nope! Way I see it, they're heading for Devil's Canyon. We should've thought of that. That canyon's like a blind hole, remember? Sliced deep into the mountain. Been used many, many times by rustlers. They moved their stolen herd in there to keep them from scattering while they set up an ambush for anybody coming in after them."

Josh looked at Jason. "What about Cougar Canyon?"

"Cougar's too far south. Besides, there's not enough flatland in there to keep a dog happy. Looks to me like they plan to leave the grassland and ride over that sandstone around Devil's Canyon," Jason said. "That's a good plan. Once there, they'll build a barricade at the mouth of the canyon and hold the herd for days, or even months, if necessary."

"Better yet," Jason added, "they'll pick out a spot high up on that canyon wall where they can knock a man out of his saddle before he even knows anybody is around."

Boone nodded. "You said the canyon is fronted by sandstone."

"Yes, sir, it is."

"I know what you're thinking," Jason said. "A good breeze or rain would wipe the sandstone clean and leave no trace of any herd or rider whatsoever."

Jason rode up and reined in close to Josh. He removed his hat and swiped a hand through his tangled hair, staring in disbelief at the deep gully ahead of them, no more than a twenty-minute ride. "Well, this ain't looking so good. We'd never make it in there without being caught in their sights. Two men with rifles could hold off a dozen on horseback. There's not a drop of cover. It's perfect—has been for years before the Pitchfork took over the lower valley."

Josh shook his head. "I think these two yahoos are building their own herd," he said.

"They're not alone," Boone said, tilting his head to the ground where they had reined their horses. Josh rode around Boone's Appaloosa for a closer look. "Where'd these come from?"

Jason dismounted to take a look at the tracks and bent over to run a hand across one of them. "Bar shoes."

"Pitchfork?"

"Right."

Boone removed his hat, looking around, surveying the land piece by piece. "We might as well hole up here," he said. "No need to rush in and catch a bullet. As long as someone remains out here, there's not much of a chance those boys will be able to move the cattle without being seen. I think I'll take a ride and check out these other tracks."

"What are we to do?"

"Just sit tight," Boone said. "Find yourself a soft spot in the shade, and keep your eyes open. I need to ride on north to the ranch and see how things are with Hoke and Mary Agnes. Don't take any chances shooting it out if they decide to move the herd. Just wait for me here. Let the herd go."

Soon after Boone rode off and disappeared over a rise, the twins rolled out their ground blankets beneath a rock overhang. Water would be no problem. There was plenty in both of their canteens. Jason had enough salt bacon and flour to last a few days, and Josh always made it one of his habits to never be without coffee and a pot to boil the grounds.

In the distance they could see Boone. "Something's wrong up there," Jason said.

"He knows it."

The rocky ledge above them kept the glare out of their eyes. Even as they measured everything around them, Jason mused aloud that Boone had selected the one spot that rendered it impossible for the rustlers to make a clean break without taking a bullet or being seen. Just as a man with a rifle on the inside could do what he wanted without taking any serious return fire.

"He's thinking of those tracks we found," Josh said. "They came right up from the Pitchfork range and crossed over those two rustlers' tracks without stopping for a look."

"Yeah, and Boone knew it," said Jason.

"You're thinking they're headed for the Double Deuce?"

"Looks that way. That has to be his reason for riding out in such a hurry."

"I've learned something about him. He ain't one to miss a trick. You notice he didn't say a lot. Just rode off like it was the thing to do." Josh gave Jason a quick glance.

"Maybe we should trail after him, keep him in our sight. If those tracks belong to Gorman's men, he'll need some help, and plenty of it."

"Maybe so, but we need to do what he asked us to in case he cuts back later on a different trail."

"What if he's late coming?"

Josh thought about Jason's question for a few seconds. "Well, then I guess we can ride."

Jason walked out from under the overhang and stood staring at the canyon across from them. "Well, I'm not up to sitting around very long doing nothing," he said. "Ain't no telling what kind of trouble Travis will run into if we're right about those tracks."

Josh couldn't help but agree with his brother, but they

could be reading too much into Boone's decision to ride on ahead.

"Look down there!"

Josh's heart skipped. He cocked his rifle. Jason was pointing toward the mouth of Devil's Canyon. A man stood there, boldly out in the open. He held a pair of binoculars to his eyes and was staring directly at the overhang.

Chapter Twelve

Mary Agnes stood on the porch, wishing to see Travis Boone riding out in front of the herd. She was alone with Hoke. Critter Malone had ridden off for Six Mile Junction after sharing breakfast, promising to take a look at Eagle Pass on his way. First, though, he wanted to make sure Boone had the cattle on the move and was riding without trouble.

Something unusual was happening to her, and she couldn't understand what it meant.

She missed a man she barely knew.

Dreams seldom bothered her, but last night's was different. Boone had been in trouble, somewhere far off. There had been smoke, and shadows, and men with guns.

When Boone left for Six Mile, the look in his gray eyes had been far more intense than usual. Something she had said to him had bothered him. There were spells when she handled people wrong and said something utterly stupid. That was a part of herself she detested.

She returned inside the house without seeing the dark line of riders moving in single file along the foothills. There were six of them—each one heavily armed, each one grim-faced as he rode north toward the Double Deuce.

Carter Sims, who was holding the point, stared straight ahead. In the past hour, after leaving the Pitchfork, he and the others had ridden steadily, with very little conversation among them. With the Double Deuce ranch house finally in sight, Nathan Wilcher rode up to Sims. "This is a bad thing we're being told to do, Carter," he said.

Sims shrugged. "What did you expect to do when you were hired, Nathan? You take orders same as all of us, or you ride off without looking back."

"Makes no difference," Nathan said. "I've got a bad feeling. What if we run into that Boone feller when we get there?"

"We won't run into him, Nathan. He's searching for his herd."

"But if he shows, what do we do then?"

"You heard Gorman. What'd he say?"

"He said kill him."

"Then that's what we'll do," Sims said.

Nathan Wilcher shook his head. "Well, I don't care for it. And there's something else. I ain't never taken no gunfight to a woman, and I ain't liking one bit what Gorman told us we were to do."

Sims said nothing, his eyes less cold. Kidnapping Mary Agnes was not his line of work either, but to go against Wells Gorman's orders wasn't on the list of things a smart man would do.

"Did you hear me, Carter?" Wilcher asked again. "That woman ain't done nothing to nobody. It's her land he's after. It's not her fault the damn river's on her land!"

"I heard you, so just shut up for a while. When she put up that barbwire fence, she signed her death warrant. She was a fool to think Gorman would let it go. What th' hell difference would a damn canal do to that lousy plot of ground?"

"Her husband is buried there!"

"Then we can move him!"

"What're we gonna do with her once we got her?"

"*You* won't do anything, damn it. Two of our boys are to take her to Dutchman's Creek and hold her there until Gorman makes whatever decision he has on his mind. If he says kill her, we'll kill her. It'll be his doing."

"I ain't riding up there, Carter. That old cabin's about to rot down."

"Nobody asked you to ride up there. Don't worry about it. You can stay here. Fact is, I would rather you found yourself a spot up there somewhere on the mountain so you can keep a sharp eye out for Boone. Once he shows, all you need to do is get on your horse and beat it back to the ranch and let Gorman know Boone's out here where we can get to him."

"What happens when she's at the Dutchman?"

"Who cares? If Boone learns where she is being kept, he'll come running, and Ham Dooley and Neal Plummer were told to take care of him the minute he shows. That's all I know."

"Dooley? I swear, Carter, that's one old man I ain't messing with, not while he has that two-edged bowie in his fist. He scares the fits out of me every time I'm around him."

"That's why we got him." Sims shrugged. They separated and rode on, Sims far ahead.

A quarter mile from the Double Deuce, with the ranch finally in sight, Sims reined up and waited for the other riders to catch up and gather around him.

"Okay. Everybody take it easy. When we get there, you do as I say, and we'll have this thing over with and be on our way without losing a man. You got that?"

A chorus of grunts was his answer.

As soon as they arrived, they checked the barn. "If that black man's anywhere around, you shoot him dead. You got that? Dead!" Sims then directed two of his men to a spot at each end of the front porch.

Inside the Double Deuce ranch house, unaware of the line of riders approaching, Hoke Canfield was out of bed and sitting at the kitchen table with a fresh cup of coffee, reading Frank J. Wilstach's story, *Wild Bill, the Prince of Pistoleers*. His dad had bought it for him a year before he was ambushed and killed. Hoke was so captivated by the story, he didn't hear a sound.

Mary Agnes sat quietly across the room. She was restless. "I wish Boone and the Parkers would get here," she said, without looking at her son.

"They will, Mom, don't worry."

At first it was the blowing of a horse. A moment later, a board on the front porch squeaked.

"Someone's out there," Hoke whispered.

Mary Agnes rushed into Hoke's bedroom for his rifle. On her way back, she grabbed the shotgun for her own use. Scrambling around in a drawer filled with clothes, she finally found a box of shells for the shotgun, which had been without shells for over a year.

She inserted two.

Hoke eased to the door, his thin body crouched over. He could hear someone breathing on the porch. His mother handed him his rifle and whispered for him to be careful.

For the first time since he was five, Hoke disregarded his mother. It was not a smart move. With a lunge, he shoved the door wide open and rushed outside—directly into the chest of a tall, startled man who was in the motion of grabbing for the door latch.

Startled, Hoke pushed the rifle hard against the man's stomach and pulled the trigger.

"Harry's shot!" The voice came from deep in the front-yard darkness.

Two other men hurtled across the porch, leaping over the downed man. Hoke did all he could to back away and escape the gun aimed at his head, but his feet became tangled, and he stumbled backward and into the arms of a man who came from around the corner of the house.

He felt the blade of a knife and gasped with horror as the razor-sharp edge cut a deep, bloody gash across his chest and then twisted and tore its way into his organs.

A man shouted. "No, no, damn it, no killing! Don't hurt that woman. Gorman wants her alive."

Hoke felt a man's rough hands grab him around the waist. He was lifted off his feet and carried across the yard, where he was shoved hard against a tree. A brittle hemp rope was wrapped around his arms and upper body and the trunk of the tree, pinioning him against the thick, crusty bark.

Chapter Thirteen

An hour before nightfall Boone thought he saw a tiny wink of orange light break through the heavily treed mountain that hovered over the Double Deuce, high up among the cedars and ponderosa pine. It would be another fifteen minutes before he got to the Canfield homeplace, and he'd keep the light in mind.

Somebody was watching.

He had ridden for what he thought was less than ten more minutes when the ranch and other small nearby structures began to take on distinct shapes. Mary Agnes should be there, he thought, when he realized the house was completely in shadows and the front door was standing wide open. Though it seemed odd, one of them—Mary Agnes or her son, Hoke—must have gone to bed without remembering to lock up.

Then shadowy shapes met his stare head-on. The Appaloosa balked, and Boone, surprised by the big stallion's sudden reaction, knew something wasn't right. "You're making me edgy, horse," Boone said aloud, kneeing the Appaloosa to keep moving at its steady pace.

He slowed the Appaloosa, bothered by what he could see of the ranch house. His stomach sank as he approached the front yard. It was far too early for Mary Agnes and Hoke to settle in for the night without leaving a light shining somewhere in the house.

Boone dismounted in the front yard so he could look around. He didn't know for sure of any real trouble, but the Appaloosa did; he felt the big animal's chest muscles tighten, heard him snort as he stepped down from the saddle. Then he saw the darker shadow that lay bunched at the foot of a large tree.

He took two cautious, uneasy steps and realized with a sudden sickness what was tied to the trunk—Hoke Canfield's slim, blood-soaked body.

He dropped to his knees beside Hoke. "No, no!" He choked and swore at the sight of the knife wounds. "Who did this?" He ripped at the grass rope with the blade of his knife until it lay twisted and bloody on the ground. "Who, son? Who did this? I have to know!"

Then—*Mary Agnes!* Where was she?

He stood up, spun around, and rushed into the house. He searched each room, including the kitchen, then returned outside and hurried to the bunkhouse and back. He searched the ground in front of the ranch house for any sign, and even in the dim light he found the deep tracks of horses with the same bar-shoe hoofprints he and the Parkers had seen near Devil's Canyon.

He swore. *Pitchfork brand!*

His lips thinned as he stood over the boy, his anger swelling like the sky at the beginning of a northeastern storm.

He stared at Hoke's blood and the frozen look on his young face. The boy had had to pay with his life so a rich man could strike fear into a woman who would never scrape and bow down to his foul desires.

If they had taken her with them, there was no way of knowing what they would do to her. If Boone's suspicions were right, Gorman had turned the first page in a deadly and personal war.

In the dark, with only a small moon's light, he buried Hoke near the willows where the swift water of the South Fork flowed. Once he was finished covering and marking the grave, he began placing creek rock neatly over the rise of rich dirt. Then he turned to stare at the mountain ridge; the light was still there, weak yet strong enough to find its way through the massive timbers.

He continued to stare. There was no movement any-where nearby, at least none that he could see from where he stood by Hoke's small grave . . . but he'd find out who was on the mountain, and why.

High up on the steep mountainside, on foot and feeling his way along the tricky terrain in the dark, revolver in his right hand, Boone made his way across several trodden animal paths and around a deep, slippery depression, obviously an old wash made by winter storms and summer rains. With the glow of the orange light still in his sight, he followed a path around a cluster of rocks. It ended abruptly.

He held his revolver muzzle down at his side when he caught the smell of smoke.

The aroma of coffee reached him as he made his way along a narrow rock bench, breathing silently. Ahead of him, the dark form of a man sat hunched over a small fire, holding a tin cup to his mouth. A rifle lay by the man's side.

Somewhere in the dimness, twigs cracked under the weight of the man's stirring horse. Boone eased closer, careful to avoid the loose rock and deadfall that lay thick over the ground. He found the horse, a young dapple-gray, tall and sinewy, tethered to the roots of an upturned tree, the Pitchfork brand embedded on the gray's left rump.

The horse tossed its head and blew nervously as Boone moved to its side toward the fire. A man's voice came immediately, soothing the animal. "Easy boy, just take it easy. Everything's fine. Nobody knows we're here."

At the sound of the man's gravelly voice, Boone stopped dead in his tracks. A man lived longer when he was vigilant, a lesson he had learned during the years before Bill Yates. He kept the barrel of his revolver pointed steadily in the direction of the man's cautious voice. A boot crunched on the deadfall, moving his way. Suddenly a slim, dark figure was in Boone's view, almost in arm's reach. The man walked to the dapple-gray, rifle in his hand. Boone heard him whisper to the gray and watched him run a hand along the nervous animal's neck. "Something botherin' you, big fella? You want me to look around some for you? It's only the wind."

The dapple-gray's head swung around.

Boone had moved out into the open and was standing with his gun in hand. "Toss your rifle and your revolver over here, mister, and do it so it doesn't make a sound, or I'll kill you where you stand."

The man dropped the rifle as if it was a snake and stood with his arms out from his hips. "Your revolver . . . now!" Boone said.

The frightened man used two fingers of his right hand to

pull the revolver from its holster, while staring at Boone. He dropped it also. "I know you—you're Travis Boone!"

"Start walking," Boone said.

There was a moment of silence. The wind fell from higher elevations.

"Please, mister, I ain't done nothing wrong. Please don't hurt me!"

"You came to kill me," Boone said.

"No, no, that's not so."

It was finally dark throughout the hillside, but the fire's small blaze gave off enough light for Boone to see the man's broad face and bushy mustache and the quivering muscle on the side of his jaw.

Boone kicked dirt over the small campfire to smother the small blaze and tilted the coffeepot, spilling the liquid on the dying embers. "Okay, now move out," he said, pointing his revolver down the hillside.

With the man in front, Boone walked the man's horse off the hillside and across the wide, clear space in front of the ranch house, where he dropped the reins of the gray to the ground and let it stand. "Who are you?" Boone asked.

"My name's Wilcher, Mr. Boone . . . Nathan Wilcher," he said. "I'm a hunter. Sorry I spooked you. I was looking for a panther what's been killing some cattle around these parts. It got cold, so I stopped to make a little fire."

"You're a liar," Boone said. "There's no panthers anywhere near this mountain, and there's no cattle for miles around. You're a Pitchfork rider."

"I—I didn't mean—" Wilcher began, but he stopped when Boone raised his revolver, his thumb hooked over the gun's hammer.

"You're one of Gorman's men?"

"Yes . . . yes, sir. I work for Wells Gorman. Two years now. He's got a lot of men. Good men. You do anything to me, you'll be sorry. . . . You'll pay—"

"Get on your horse," Boone said, reaching for the coiled rope lashed to Wilcher's saddle and nodding at the horse. "Up!" he said.

Reluctantly, Wilcher stepped forward. He put his left boot into the stirrup and stepped up and into the saddle. He sat slumped forward with his hands resting on top of the saddle horn, staring at the rope Boone held.

"What're you going to do with that rope?"

Boone shook out the rope, and while Wilcher watched, he began forming a hangman's noose. When he finished, he held it up in the moonlight and studied it, then said, "That looks like a good, strong noose to me. How's it look to you?"

Wilcher yelled, "Hey, what's that for?"

"I'm calling it a Pitchfork noose. You make one move I don't like, and I'll put a hole in your head."

Wilcher's face drained. "Wait just a minute! You can't— what'd I do?"

"You rode up here with a bunch of murdering scum. A young man is buried over there by that tree. He was killed for no reason at all, and his mother was taken from her home as their prisoner—and now you're about to learn a priceless lesson."

"No, no, please, I wasn't even down here when all that happened. I was just a lookout. . . . I was told to keep an eye out for you. That's the truth! I swear. I didn't come up here to hurt nobody."

"Where'd they take Mary Agnes?"

Wilcher hesitated. "I don't know." He took a deep breath. "They took her with them."

"Where?"

"I swear I don't know."

Boone pushed the barrel of his revolver into the soft spot just above the man's belt. "What did you say?"

"Okay, okay, they have orders from Mr. Gorman to kill her if you try anything. Ham knows how to handle a woman."

"Who?"

"Ham Dooley. It was him who hurt that boy you buried. I didn't see it happen, but I heard the boy scream once or twice—Ham did it for the fun of it. That's the kind of man he is. You'll know him when you see him. He's a squatty little man, bald as a hen's egg."

The Pitchfork rider's words hit Boone like a sudden splash of ice water. His heart skipped a beat, and he had to struggle with his anger. Hoke had been beaten thoroughly, dragged across the yard and butchered, and left to bleed to death lashed to the trunk of a tree.

Boone stared at Wilcher. "I'm going to ask you one more time. Where'd they take Mary Agnes?"

"I don't know for sure—"

"You're lying again," Boone said, shoving the revolver barrel hard once again into Wilcher's ribs.

"Wait . . . I think they plan to hold her in an abandoned shack. There's one on Dutchman's Creek that Gorman owns. They're to keep her there until he comes for her. After that, I don't know what they will do with her."

"Where's Dutchman's Creek?"

"Its way south of here, high up, maybe ten miles on the mountain. Getting there without being seen ain't no easy thing for a man on a horse to do."

"How many men did Gorman send up there?"

"Just two—Dooley and Neal Plummer. That's all I know.

I'm sorry. All the others rode back to the Pitchfork." The frightened man's voice quavered. "I'd stay here if I was you. They'll be back and burn this place down. I heard them talking about it. You just wait."

Once Boone had Wilcher settled in his saddle, he reached for the gray's reins and tossed them around the saddle horn so they would hang loose.

"What're you doing?"

"I'm giving your horse a loose rein so he can go where he knows best."

"I can handle him. I don't need a loose rein."

"Not this time."

Wilcher stared at Boone as though he had something more to say to him, but he remained very still and kept his mouth closed. At least that was how it appeared—until Boone stretched out the loop of the noose and slipped it over Wilcher's head. He brought the other end of the rope down and under the gray's belly, laced it through the two cinch rings of the Texas rig, and knotted the rope in a slipknot.

Boone raised the Walker Colt. "Stretch your arms behind your back. Do it now!"

Wilcher reluctantly did as he was told. Boone wrapped Wilcher's wrists with three loops of a rawhide saddle string he had cut from the horse's saddle. He stepped back, holding his revolver at his side. "Now give that horse a couple heels and get moving. Let it have its head."

The last Boone saw of Nathan Wilcher, the dapple-gray was making its way slowly along the foothills and heading due south.

He went to the bunkhouse and began packing all the provisions he could find, then returned to the ranch house.

There he gathered extra blankets from the bedrooms; in the kitchen he found several air-tights of peaches and string beans, a hunk of beef, sliced salt bacon, and a brown paper bag of ground coffee.

Behind his saddle he tied a rolled-up buffalo coat he found hanging in a closet, along with a second heavy sheepskin coat with a large fur collar. He filled a war bag with enough ammunition for a standoff fight.

As he had done many, many times before, he'd use the element of surprise—just like the militant Sioux Red Cloud, who'd cleared the Bozeman Trail of the white man's forts.

Strike first, and strike hard.

Early the next morning, after an intense search across the face of the mountain, high up near the rim where the trees thinned out, Boone found the cave he had been searching for. It was large and roomy, and although some distance from the Double Deuce, it was high enough on the mountain to keep the entire valley in his sight and difficult to attack from either side. Whoever found the cave would be forced to come straight through its narrow opening.

If someone did find the opening, he hoped it would be Wells Gorman.

By midmorning Boone was feeling anxious. He had ridden more than five miles, across small mountain streams, over dark and dangerous landslides, and around deep washouts, before finding the massive cave. He'd unpacked all the provisions, utensils, food, bedroll, extra blankets, ten boxes of ammunition, and a supply of wooden matches he'd found in the Canfields' kitchen. He placed the buffalo coat and sheepskin on a ground blanket and looked around for the most likely place to build a fire so he could have something in his stomach before his ride to Dutchman's Creek.

He thought of Wilcher's words: *They have orders to kill her if you try anything.*

Well, if that happened, they would soon be stepping over their own dead.

That was his vow.

Chapter Fourteen

Mary Agnes sat on the cabin floor with her back to a wall. She was frightened but determined not to show her captors any of her fear and anger. Her wrists were lashed tightly with rawhide thongs, but her arms were in her lap, free to move.

She kept her eyes from those of her captors.

Although she remained observant of their demeanor, her thoughts were not of herself but of her son, Hoke. She had heard him cry out and knew they had killed him. She heard the men celebrating and prayed silently for a chance to strike them both dead.

Across the room, the two men sat at a small table playing two-hand poker—a young man in his late twenties called Neal Plummer, and a wrinkle-faced old man who kept gawking and grinning at her, his small green eyes gleaming with desire as he inspected her body, inch by inch.

She knew him. Ham Dooley. She'd seen him twice before, once during one of Gorman's trips to her ranch before he spoke of his need for water.

103

The ride to Dutchman's Creek had been long. Plummer had ridden out front, seldom looking back, Dooley riding behind her, making her skin crawl.

There had been many moments during that ride when she seriously considered making a break at the first chance, but by the end of the long day she realized the improbability of escaping, because she was unfamiliar with this part of the mountain and its many animal trails. But by her very nature, she refused to allow herself to lose all hope.

She hadn't dared to sleep. Before the sun had risen for another day of her confinement, Dooley and Plummer were already at odds with each other, threatening to bash heads. A big part of their conversation included her. She heard that Gorman wanted to have his men draw Boone to Dutchman's Creek so he could come in behind him with Carter Sims and kill him. Apparently Wells Gorman would be a part of the plan. He'd want it to be personal.

At the small table, Dooley laid out three nines and grinned wickedly at Plummer and his two jacks. "You know something, Plummer?"

"What's that?"

"Besides being a lousy poker player, you don't know a blame thing about women. Now, that woman over there against the wall is about as fine a woman a man could ever put his eyes on."

"Yeah, well, it don't matter none. She don't belong to you."

"She could."

"She ain't looking kindly at you, Ham. So don't go getting your hopes up."

For a long time Dooley just stared across the table at Plummer. Finally, he said, "I bet you ain't never had a real woman in your whole life."

"You don't know nothing about what I've had."

"Ha! I know that much by just looking at you."

Mary Agnes learned by listening to every spoken word. It was obvious that Plummer was not a close friend of Dooley's, and Plummer had made it clear he planned to leave the Pitchfork as soon as he had his first paycheck in his hip pocket and a horse that knew how to run on hard ground.

"You need to remember, Ham," Plummer said. "She's out of your loop, and you better leave her be, or Gorman will take that blacksnake whip to you like he did McNabb."

Dooley grunted and stood up. He sauntered to the front door, still carrying his smirk along with him. He shoved the door open and looked outside, swearing into the dark. Rain was falling and turning into icy sleet. "Gorman ain't comin'. He's still sittin' in his big ol' ranch house warming his butt while we're holed up here with a storm coming down on us. I'd say you and me need to get out of here while the getting's good. Maybe I'll saddle up an' leave you like a horse with a broken leg."

"You won't, old man, so keep your mouth shut before I shut it for you. We're staying right here like Gorman told us. Don't worry about that Boone feller showing up. If he's got any sense at all, he's halfway back to Montana."

"You're both stupid," Mary Agnes blurted suddenly. "He'll find us, and you'll pay for what you did to my son!"

Plummer shrugged. "I'm sorry about your son, ma'am, but he was in a fight. People get killed. That's the way it is. Don't you worry none about Dooley, though. He puts a hand on you, I'll shoot him."

With a grunt, he shoved his chair from the table and stood up and stared at Mary Agnes, then walked to the stove and filled a cup with steaming coffee and brought it back to the table.

Dooley leered at her. Plummer glared at him. "You old filthy fool, you better leave her be! That's the last time I'm telling you." Holding the coffee cup in his left hand, he let his right hand rest on the butt of his gun, while he sipped his coffee.

Mary Agnes saw Dooley's silly grin turn hard and vicious. He'd kill Plummer without blinking, she thought, and then what would happen to her?

Carter Sims thought Wells Gorman had made the biggest mistake of his life when he allowed Ham Dooley within a mile of Mary Agnes Canfield.

Sims was not an empathetic man and didn't really care what Gorman had in mind for Mary Agnes Canfield, but putting a woman of *any* age in the same room with Ham Dooley was like hiring a hungry fox to guard a henhouse.

He told Gorman as much. "I'm telling you, Wells, we need to go up to the Dutchman and bring that woman down here before Dooley gets his paws on her."

"Not just yet," Gorman said. "We have time. Dooley won't lay a hand on her. Plummer will take care of that. I told him about Dooley and his knife-cutting ways, and if things got out of hand, he was to shoot the old devil in the crotch. Right now I want Travis Boone to stick his head out so we can cut it off," Gorman said. "I want him long gone or dead—makes no difference which. Once he finds out we've got Mary Agnes, he'll be on the hunt. All I need to do is scatter some men along the mountain. Keep them moving so he won't have any idea what's going on until it's too late."

Sims yawned and complained of being dead tired and

needing rest, but Gorman meant what he had said, and finally Sims went along with it.

There'd be no rest.

Besides, Gorman was wearing his Smith & Wesson on his hip, with the thong off, something he'd not done for years. Sims knew he meant business.

"My plan with Mary Agnes is still the same as it was yesterday. She's going to sign over that small piece of Eagle Pass to me like I want, so we can get the canal in operation before winter sets in for good. When that's done, you can forget the Double Deuce ever existed."

"What about Creed?"

"If we have to dig him up, that's what we'll do. Toss what's left of him into the river. Just get him out of my way."

They rode north into the slanting sleet that came down the Laramie until late that afternoon, at which point Gorman had Sims ride ahead to search for any sign that Boone had driven the Double Deuce herd through the gap and had used the small valley to get the herd back onto Canfield land.

"What about the Parker boys?"

"Let 'em be."

Sims left Gorman and rode in a looping pattern so as not to overlook any signs that Travis Boone was anywhere within shooting distance of them. For more than an hour he crossed and recrossed the scrub-free land, searching intently for a big Appaloosa's tracks, until finally he found evidence of Boone in the soft mud along the foothills, but no sign of cattle being anywhere near.

Off to the east, three shadows that could only be early-rising buzzards circled a far-off ridge. Sims stared at them. Below the three buzzards he saw dark smoke rising and spreading over a long, treeless ridge.

He waited for Gorman to ride toward him. "There's some tracks, a lone horse," he told Gorman once he rode up, "moving north for the Double Deuce."

Gorman swore. "Then he must know we have Mary Agnes."

"I'd say he does," Sims said.

"Okay," Gorman said. "Let's hope he's on his way to Dutchman's Creek so we can come in behind him and nail him to a tree."

Sims pointed to the buzzards and smoke. "I think he's already been there."

Gorman stared at the drifting smoke. "You left Nathan at the Deuce, didn't you?"

"Yes, sir. He's got a spot up on that hill."

"Well, he was to warn us. You see any sign of him?"

"No, sir."

"Well, let's get out of here," Gorman said, twisting his horse around. "I've got a bad feeling about this place. We'll ride up to the Dutchman and check on that cloud of smoke. First, though, we need to find Clay Fisher and the Mex."

It was late in the afternoon when Wells Gorman rode down a narrow, weed-choked, wagon-rutted street with three standing buildings abandoned for more years than either man could remember. Besides Carter Sims, Wells brought a new man named Lonny Nash with him. Clay Fisher and Santa Fe tracker Juan Joaquin were waiting for them in front of what remained of a gristmill.

Gorman dismounted and said, "Okay, it looks like Boone's on the prowl. Sims and I will ride up to the Dutchman. You two stay here, maybe take a ride a ways to check some of the places where a rider might have crossed the valley. If either of you see any sign of Boone, make sure you let him ride on through, as long as it looks like he's heading for the Dutchman."

"A thousand pardons, *patrón,*" said Juan Joaquin.

Gorman swung around, staring. "What is it, Juan?"

"Why am I to stay off the mountain?"

"Because I told you to."

"I thought you hired me to track the man you call Boone and kill him. You promised you would pay me a good bonus."

Gorman shot him a sullen glance. "All right! You do what you want. Nash, you stay here with Fisher. You'll know what to do if Boone shows his face."

Joaquin nodded. "Thank you so much, Señor Wells."

Clay Fisher kept his silence. This wasn't his fight. He hadn't been hired on as a gunfighter, but right now he was caught in the middle. He was owed a month's salary, and once he had that in his pocket, he would be gone like a flight of geese heading south.

"Okay," Gorman said. "Now here's the full picture. Sims and I aim to bring Mary Agnes back to the ranch. If we haven't dealt with Boone by then, it'll be your job to keep him from crossing over this part of the mountain until we return. You got that?"

Fisher nodded.

"Okay," Gorman said. "That's settled. You two can ride out sometime tomorrow."

Joaquin turned away and stepped into the saddle of his horse and rode for the mountain, grinning widely. Gorman was pleased he had a tracker as good as the Mexican. The man knew plenty about the mountain, and he didn't let it scare him as it did Sims. Gorman had sent him up there time after time just to learn the caves, trails, and sparse ridges. It would be a challenge for a good hunter.

"Look at that, Carter." Gorman grinned as Joaquin rode and disappeared into the underbrush at the foot of the mountain. "That damn Mex can't wait to get his hands on Boone."

Chapter Fifteen

Travis Boone had a problem with the winter sun. He wasn't worried about being able to find the cabin where Gorman's men had taken Mary Agnes, but he preferred a dimly lit trail once he arrived. There were many sparse areas on the mountain where a rider would be out in the open for a few minutes. Even from such a great distance, the sunlight would make him an easy target.

All it would take would be one lonely rifle shot, a man of keen eye, and a fine old Remington slide-action.

Boone was surprised. Why had Gorman ordered his men to kill Hoke and kidnap Mary Agnes, then take her to some secluded mountain cabin and hold her there? Certainly it was not a move that would endear Gorman to Mary Agnes. Gorman must have reached a point of frustration with Mary Agnes. As it was, she would never allow Gorman's men to set foot on Eagle Pass land—and Gorman knew it as he knew his own name.

By the time Boone found the Dutchman, it was nearly dark. He switched trails and rode down a steep slope that put him a yard or so from the cabin's only window, where he dismounted a few feet to the rear. Inside, a small, flickering light barely made it through the coat of filth that coated the glass. Mary Agnes, sitting in silence across the room, gazed up at him with no visible reaction.

Good for you, Mary Agnes, good for you!

The cabin was smaller than Boone had thought it would be. It had only one room, occupied by two men who sat at a small table in the middle. One was short and bald. He had to be Ham Dooley, if Wilcher had told him the truth. That meant the younger man was Neal Plummer.

Boone continued to peer through the window. In front of Mary Agnes, who had her back to the wall, was a small kerosene lamp with its wick turned down low. Off to her right, a red-belly woodstove was being fed two pieces of kindling by Ham Dooley. He had left the table for a cup of coffee, and, after pouring his cup full, he picked up the wood and jammed it into the stove, then stood back, dusting his hands.

Mary Agnes must feel terrible, Boone thought. And the night was not over.

Boone had to make a decision and do something quickly. The cabin was flat-roofed, small, and had animal-hide hinges on the front door, which meant the door opened outward rather than inward, which would harm Boone's chances for a sudden entrance.

Silently, he led his horse back off the trail and up above the cabin out of the mushy ground, so it would be unseen if either of the men decided to check on their own horses or stroll outside for a breath of cool night air.

The weather had changed within the last hour. It was colder, and the small amount of rain that filtered through the tangled mass of timber around him was beginning to turn into sleet, pelting Boone on the back of his neck. He moved back to the small window so he could catch the two men at the table with their backs to the front door.

All he could think of was how to get Mary Agnes out of the cabin without her being hurt. It was not going to be easy. He would need to make certain exactly where Dooley and Plummer were standing or sitting. He didn't know how dangerous Plummer was, but Dooley—any man who would cut up Hoke the way he had would be worth watching. He first thought of stampeding both men's horses, with the hope that the sound of the horses making a break would spring the men out the front door and into his arms. But he dismissed that thought.

Leaning against the outside wall, a few feet from the window, he thought he heard the two men complaining. "Storm's coming. You hear it, Plummer? We're gonna be holed up here for a month if we ain't out of here before daylight!"

"Can't be helped," the younger one said. "We can't go nowhere with that woman. We gotta be here like Gorman told us to."

"We can leave her here. Who the hell would care?"

"You know we can't do that. She'd starve for sure."

"Let her starve," Dooley answered angrily. Then, dealing the ace and king of spades from the bottom of the deck, he smiled and said, "I guess we could lay 'round and wait for Boone to show. Maybe I could cut a slice out of him to soften him up for Gorman. Whaddya think about that, Mr. Plummer?"

Plummer remained silent. He reached across the table and picked up the two cards Dooley had slipped from the bottom of the deck and slid them between the three cards he held in his hand.

"I'll play these."

Dooley began to swear.

Plummer laughed for the first time.

Dooley's swearing sounded like a pig squealing. He shoved a chair across the room with his foot and stared at Plummer. "Maybe when this is all over, I'll cut on you a little bit. Just to keep in shape. How's that grab you?"

"You'd have to do it in my sleep." Plummer stood up and stalked to the door. "I'll check on the horses," he said as he shoved open the door, stomped outside, and rounded the corner of the cabin.

If he saw Boone standing in the dark with his back to the cabin wall, it was only for a split second before Boone raised his rifle and dropped Plummer to the ground, his head landing at an odd angle.

Only Mary Agnes knew of Plummer's sudden downfall. She had seen Boone twice peering through the small window, and now her eyes were on the door, knowing Boone would be coming for Dooley next.

"What was that noise? Is that damn fool shooting at varmints in the dark?" Dooley said, shoving his chair away from the table and standing, staring at Mary Agnes, as if it were her fault.

She shrugged and remained silent.

When the door swung open, Dooley kept leering at her and didn't even turn around.

He growled, "All right, Plummer, git some money on the table. I'm gonna skin you out of yore last nickel."

Ham Dooley was reaching for the cards when Boone stepped through the open door with his revolver raised. Dooley spun around and cursed. Then he grabbed for the table and shoved it toward Boone, sending the kerosene lamp sliding off and onto the floor, spilling kerosene in puddles at his feet.

"What the—?"

Boone shot Dooley point-blank in the middle of the chest. The Walker's bullet lifted the bald man up onto his toes and then sent him sprawling over backward.

Suddenly the kerosene exploded into red and orange flames, spreading quickly across the floor. In no time the room was a mass of flames and smoke.

Mary Agnes was on her feet and scrambling around Dooley's outstretched body as Boone stepped past her and stuck the barrel of his Walker into Dooley's mouth.

"This is for Hoke Canfield!"

Mary Agnes screamed. "No!"

Boone shot him. The sound was like that of a lightning strike. Dooley's body jerked once before becoming very still.

Black smoke began to fill the small cabin. Flames reached for the ceiling, spreading across the space between the wall and table until reaching for Dooley's supine body, then consuming his unwashed shirt. The smell of burning flesh and hair filled the room. Boone grabbed Mary Agnes and pulled her out the door.

Outside, he cut the rawhide strings from her wrists, and she threw her arms around him. All her orderliness and self-discipline appeared to fade, and huge tears filled her eyes and streamed down her cheeks.

Boone had never seen her cry.

"Oh, Travis, he killed my son! I heard—"

Boone could only nod. He didn't know what he could say that would help her, so he just drew her away from the cabin as the roof caved in. "I buried him, ma'am," he said breathlessly.

"On the Deuce?"

"Yes."

The rain mixed with sleet moved over Dutchman's Creek and on down the mountain to the east, but in the time it took to pass over the creek, the slick coat of ice that had formed on tree limbs began to melt and drip like rain. The cabin continued to burn.

Boone found Mary Agnes' pinto standing outside an untouched hovel, its bridle reins dragging on the ground. The other two horses had broken loose from the hovel and disappeared somewhere into the timber.

Boone said, "Gorman will see that smoke a mile away." He glanced at Mary Agnes. Astonishingly, her profile was calm now, and her body was poised; her courage, Boone thought, had returned. "Where will we go?" she asked him softly.

"There's a cave," he said dryly. "We need to stay away from the ranch for a while. That'll be the first place they look."

"Of course," Mary Agnes said with a deep sigh.

Boone rode out in front of her and the pinto. Ham Dooley was scum, but Boone still knew that he would, at some time, have to make peace with himself for shooting the bastard. Killing a man that way, with no chance to defend himself, wasn't his style. And he had no way of knowing how Mary Agnes felt about it. Later he would make peace with her. That was the first thing he would do.

Yet killing Dooley had not been a difficult choice for him. Not with the memory of Hoke Canfield's violated body burned deeply into his mind.

Chapter Sixteen

When Carter Sims and Wells Gorman crossed Dutchman's Creek, all they found was a pile of charred timber and a dapple-gray horse standing over Nathan Wilcher, its head down, legs spread.

Wilcher lay on the ground with his wrists tied behind his back and a noose drawn tightly against his left ear. The other end of the rope was still threaded through the two cinch rings of his saddle.

"Boone!"

Sims sprang from his saddle with his knife in his hand and slashed the rawhide from the cinch rings and pulled Wilcher's body from beneath the gray horse, shooing the animal out of his way. "Boone did this!" Sims' throat was dry. "He knew Nathan would fall off sooner or later, and he knew when he did, he'd hang himself!"

Gorman didn't look at Nathan. He was staring at a pair of boots protruding from the rubble of charred wood. "I can't believe this is the work of one man. These were fighting men, Sims. How could Boone do this? How could one man sneak in here without being seen and kill two of my best fighting men?"

"I warned them, Wells. I told them Boone was a man who'd draw their blood without giving them a kind word, but they wouldn't listen to me!" Sims shouted. "I tried to tell you and Snowden to leave the man be. You saw what he did to Stiles. That should've warned all of us that he was a lot more than just a bronco peeler."

Gorman shrugged indifferently. He stared around, his gaze passing over the pile of black ashes the same way it would a field of corn. No emotion showed. "Looks to me like Plummer came outside for some reason and got himself killed," he said, pointing to the boots sticking out from beneath the ashes. "I'd know those boots anywhere."

"He got 'em one at a time," Sims mumbled, amazed at the deed. "These two were professionals. No man should have been able to sneak up on them. The man's telling us we're in for a war of *his* making, not ours!"

"C'mon, you think we're unable to handle one man?" Gorman said, staring hard at Sims.

Sims straightened in the saddle. "Let me put it this way, Wells. We haven't fared so well as it now stands. It's just possible we've kicked the wrong wolf."

Gorman glared at Sims and changed the subject. "Why'd the gray come here instead of the ranch, you reckon?"

"That was Dooley's old horse. He sold it to Nathan a couple months back."

"So?"

"Well, Dooley spent lot of his time up here hunting and living like a hermit. Seems daft, but the gray probably thought he was going home."

Gorman agreed grudgingly. Mentally, he counted his

men: Ed Snowden was beaten into humiliation and wasn't worth a red cent, Harlan Stiles had turned chicken after his encounter with Boone, Nathan Wilcher got his neck stretched, Ham Dooley was cooked like a Thanksgiving turkey, and Neal Plummer, the one man Gorman trusted, had gotten his neck broken without putting up a fight.

"All dead or run out of the territory. We might as well forget Kerns. He's probably on his way back to Texas right now."

Gorman had held no real liking for scum like Ham Dooley, but Plummer—now, he was another matter. Plummer was not a paid killer. He was more like a son to Gorman, although he didn't know it.

Sims was mounted. "What now?" he asked, worried.

"It looks like we're in for a long winter of killing."

Sims' face was expressionless. "Who do we start killing?"

"Don't get in a hurry, Sims. First we need some help."

"I didn't think that would ever happen."

Gorman stared at the ashes. "Who in his right mind would ever guess some bronco rider from Montana could stir up so much trouble? Anyway, you ride back to the ranch and bring every man you can dig up, even if you have to ride to Six Mile. I want that Double Deuce ranch house lit up like a grass fire. Burn it to a pile of cinders, then get out and look for Kerns while you're at it. Find out where he rode off to. I was wrong about him."

Sims shrugged. "I don't think he's anywhere around, Wells. He saddled up early—rode off and didn't say where he was going or when he'd return."

"Well, forget about him, then! We'll ride to the Canfield ranch. If we don't find Boone there, we'll split up and scatter some men over the mountain until we root him out!"

Sims glanced at the sky and shook his head at the mass

of dark clouds hanging over the valley. "This snow's gonna turn into a blizzard 'fore we know it. If we spread out and start looking for Boone in this weather, he'll pick us off one by one. We need to find some way to flush him off that mountain and get him out in the open."

"Wasn't that our first order of business?" Gorman scowled. "He blew that all to hell! Now we'll do it my way."

"But—"

"No *but*s about it," Gorman snapped. "That's final."

Carter Sims had always feared the mountains. Narrow trails, deep shadows, panthers, cougars, bears—and a general belief that something evil lay in wait beyond each rim or cave. Maybe even some upset Cheyenne or Sioux who needed a scalp to prove his worth as a man or a warrior.

"There's only one man we've got that can find Boone or kill him," Sims said. "One man."

Gorman grunted and made a wolfish smile. "You're talking about the Mex?"

"That's right."

Chapter Seventeen

At midmorning Boone and Mary Agnes rode through the mountain cave's vast entrance. Mary Agnes stared in awe at the size of the place. "I'm really amazed," she said. "How did you find this place?"

"Luck."

The cave's ceiling towered over man and woman and horse, and from what Mary Agnes could tell from where she stood, the cave drove deeply into the belly of the mountain—how far she did not know. She looked at Boone with a new awareness.

"You found this cave? I didn't know such a cave existed," she said with a laugh. "What do we do now?"

"First I'll build a fire. Later we'll figure out how we can reach the sheriff and Pete Judd. Hopefully the weather will let up some."

"You think Gorman will send his men up here after us?" she asked Travis after she was settled close to the fire he had started. "If he does, we won't have a chance."

"He'd be a fool not to," Boone said. "He doesn't like to

lose, but we'll worry about that later. Right now I need a strong cup of coffee."

Boone thought about telling her the truth. Of course they were in danger; there was little doubt about that. They could both die. But he decided it was best to keep those thoughts to himself. She had more than enough on her mind. She probably didn't realize that Wells Gorman actually planned to kill her himself. Otherwise he wouldn't have had his men take her to some out-of-the-way cabin. She had, in her own way, destroyed much more of the man than she realized. Eagle Pass meant riches to him; it meant respect, and in his eyes she had denied him that.

"Don't worry, we'll be fine," he said. "I'll see to that."

Mary Agnes listened, but she was not fooled by his assurance. She knew he was thinking of her safety, and only hers, and that made her feel like a young girl again. "I need to tell you something, Travis," she said, her eyes wide.

"It can wait," he replied.

She shook her head impatiently. "No, this is important to me. I had no doubt you would come for me, and while I waited, I prayed you would kill both those men, especially Ham Dooley. I'm sorry. I was a selfish woman. I learned of your past life soon after you arrived, but it didn't matter to me. I've been wrong about a lot of things, but I've never been wrong about the kind of man you are. I guess I just let Creed's death turn me into a spiteful woman."

Boone was about to say something about his feelings for her, but he held back. That could wait. It was best that it did. There would be another time. He hoped.

"Did Critter tell you about my past?"

"No. When you shot Gorman's man, Harlan Stiles, I knew then you had lived another life. Only a man of great experience would have been so calculated . . . so unexpected . . . and so fair."

Boone felt a chill, and gathered up loose stones and placed them in a half circle where the wall of the cave curved inward. Then he built another fire with the stones around it, positioned so they would reflect the fire's heat back into the cave yet keep the light hidden from prying eyes, at least from below on the valley floor. Inside the circle of stones he heaped dried sticks.

"I've not killed a helpless man before, ma'am."

"Ham Dooley was not helpless," she assured him.

Later Boone removed the saddle from both the pinto and the Appaloosa. He cut up an old Army blanket and rubbed both horses down.

Mary Agnes watched all his movements. "I'm so glad you came to the Deuce, Travis."

Boone slowly turned to face her. When his eyes found hers, he shook his head. "You might change your mind before this thing's over with," he said.

"That's not at all likely," she said. "Of course that could depend on how long we have to stay holed up in a cave," she added with a fresh smile.

"How about some coffee and salt bacon?" He found the salt bacon and placed half a dozen pieces in a frying pan and set it on the fire beside the coffeepot.

"You said you were lucky to find this cave. You think one of Gorman's men might be as lucky?"

"I hope not, but somebody surely does," he replied. "I doubt anybody on the Pitchfork ever made it this far up the mountain."

"I hope not," she agreed.

"Somebody's been here before, though. Just look around at the work that's been done on the cave. Probably some hunter."

Boone placed some salt bacon on a tin dish and handed it to her along with a cup of coffee. Outside, the rainy sleet had turned to snow, some blowing into the cave's entrance.

"Maybe the snow's coming at the right time for us," Mary Agnes said. "Hopefully it will force Gorman and his men to look for shelter and leave us alone for a while. Maybe we should search for another place."

"We've got time." Boone stared at the fire. Experience had warned Boone many times before not to sink into a false sense of security. That was exactly the sort of mistake Wells Gorman would be banking on.

He sipped his coffee and smiled at Mary Agnes. "Sometime tomorrow I'll take a look for as many of Gorman's men as I can locate. I think it's time for me to break up that mob. As they say, separate the little men from the big man."

"There's too many of them, Travis," she said. "And he'll hire more."

"You're probably right, but at least there'll be enough to keep me busy," he said with a smile.

"I think it's wonderful up here," Mary Agnes murmured, gazing across the fire at him. "I'm so glad we're together."

Her laugh was soft, her large blue eyes unwavering. "I feel safe, now, Travis. There were many times in that cabin when I prayed to die; then I saw your face in that small window. What a wonderful sight it was!"

Gently, he reached out his hand and let it rest on her shoulder, hearing the sharp intake of her breath. Her face blurred as she turned and put one arm behind his neck. He kissed her on her forehead and softly on her lips, and then he eased free of her.

But as his emotions soared, he thought of her son being murdered, dragged from her home, and a rich man wanting her killed.

Boone felt he had no place in her thoughts.

Why would he even think she would ever want another man in her life? She had told him as much the day he was hired, and he had no reason to believe she had changed her mind.

Yet she did not move from his side.

Chapter Eighteen

The first snow finally roared its way out of Montana and down the Laramie into Wyoming with a vengeance, falling from low-hanging dark clouds and carried by a freezing wind, pushing hard against Tommy Kerns' back as he searched the mountain for Travis Boone and Mary Agnes Canfield.

He followed a marked trail along a narrow bench until he came to a copse where he could scrutinize the valley and keep an eye open for Gorman, should he be coming out of the south.

Despite his recent trips onto the ridges and gullies of the mountain, Kerns had forgotten how slow-going the inclines under even a light snow could be. Even his horse, a long-legged black, a good, strong animal with enough common sense to find its own way over treacherous animal trails, was finding its footing difficult.

The cave Tommy Kerns searched for was three miles farther ahead at his best estimate. It was a cave of immense size, where a man and woman could hide beside a warm fire and feel safe from the searching eyes of hunting men.

Kerns had been there. It was absolutely perfect.

After another hour of searching and remembering, Kerns decided to dismount. He tied the black to a small pine out of the wind, then worked his way along the slope to where he expected to find an overhang of lichen-covered rock holding fast to every flake of falling snow.

It was there, of course, somewhere below, in one of nature's finest fissures. He expected to find what he came for—a mulish man and a kind woman, all snug and cuddly as two bugs in a rug.

He'd find them before Wells Gorman and his men riding below on the valley floor did, moving slowly north, looking in all the wrong places, four riders bunched together, collars pulled up and bodies leaning into the wind and falling snow.

Kerns spotted Gorman riding out front, as usual. Of the other riders, only Carter Sims and Clay Fisher were recognizable from the distance.

As he feared, the Mexican, Juan Joaquin, was not among them. He'd been turned loose.

Soon the riders were out of Kerns' sight. He returned to his horse and unrolled a mackinaw and shrugged into it. Winter had brought a dangerous change to the mountain, and those landmarks he had depended upon when he arrived months ago were no longer as clear. There were places, new places, where the mountain dropped abruptly straight down. No man or horse could approach from any direction without being seen. It was a drop of two thousand feet if not more and came to a sudden, crunching end in a field of boulders.

Finally he was where he had been before. He recognized the spot and caught the fragrance of smoke in his nostrils.

Wood smoke!

Someone *was* in the cave below him, and with a fire

burning. For an instant he felt like shouting to them, but the *click* of a gun hammer being pulled back changed his mind. He froze, his hands hanging rigidly at his sides. "Easy with the gun, Travis," he said. "I'm here as a peaceful man."

"Who are you?"

"Tommy Kerns."

"Okay. Come in slowly. Keep your hands where I can see them." Travis Boone stepped out from a point beyond the cave, rifle in hand. He had found the black tied to a tree branch and had brought the horse along with him.

"What brought you up here, Kerns?"

"I have a message for you."

Boone lowered his rifle and stepped back for Kerns to enter the cave. "You know Mary Agnes is here, don't you?"

Kerns nodded and removed his hat. "Howdy, ma'am. Sorry I startled you folks. I just thought you and Mr. Boone should know that Wells Gorman is still out there looking for the two of you."

"How many?" Boone asked.

"Hard to tell from up here. But you've cut into his supply of men, and that trouble at Devil's Canyon gave him an upset stomach. But he's always got a way of finding enough men to do his dirty work."

"What about you?" Boone asked.

"I'm no longer with the Pitchfork. At least in my mind, I'm not. Once the weather breaks, I'm heading for Waco as fast as my horse will take me."

"What about Devil's Canyon?" Boone asked. "What happened up there?"

"Those two Parker boys who were helping you with the Deuce herd got tired of waiting for you and went in after Mary Agnes' cattle. There was a lot of shooting going on."

"Where'd you hear that?"

"Morgan Hays . . . day 'fore yesterday. I was in Six Mile getting my horse some new shoes for the long trip back to Texas. Morgan said the sheriff rode down to tell Gorman he had a couple of his men in jail, but Gorman wasn't there."

"The Tate boys okay?"

"Not a scratch on either one of them," Kerns said.

"Any word on Critter Malone?"

"You talking about that big black man?"

Boone nodded.

"I guess that was him I saw talking with Sheriff Johnson and his deputy, Judd. They seemed to be agreeing on some things, then I heard about the Canfield boy being killed, and I gambled you'd be here rather than anywhere near the ranch. Of course they burned the ranch down, you know." Kerns held out both hands over the fire, gazing wistfully at the coffeepot. "Winter's not a good time for a war."

Boone said, "Coffee?"

"Yes. Thanks." He turned and smiled at Mary Agnes. She held out a cup to him. "I'd appreciate being able to stay here with you folks until this storm lets up some."

Boone was not yet at ease with Kerns. "I'm still curious, Kerns. Why'd you decide to warn us?"

"After what you did at the Dutchman, Gorman went berserk. He's called in a Santa Fe Mexican tracker, a professional, who will find this cave sooner or later. Maybe he has already. I had hoped the snow would cover my tracks."

"Mexican? Alone?"

"Just him an' that two-barreled shotgun he sleeps with."

Boone looked quickly to Mary Agnes. She looked so calm.

Chapter Nineteen

Juan Joaquin hated the Wyoming snow and its evil winds even more than he hated Anglos. Out of the reach of the wind and snow, he sat beneath a large rock overhang with a small fire, glaring down on the valley through a wide gap in the trees. From a small goatskin pouch he found some jerky to chew on and a half-smoked cigar to kill the taste of the jerky. Large snowflakes fell over the mountain, fluttering through the limbs of the pine trees, forcing him to add dry sticks to his small fire. He had followed another man's horse tracks, from the northern pasture of the Pitchfork to the mountain.

His smile broadened. He felt magnificent.

Wells Gorman had offered him good money to find a man and a woman he wanted killed.

It wouldn't be much longer.

He checked the nail heads that he kept handy in his coat pocket for special jobs. Not many shotguns could shoot a fistful of nail heads over and over, but this one was primed to go.

130

He stood and pulled his long coat tightly around him. There was a cave up ahead, a large cave, high up on the mountain. He'd make it there soon. All he had to do was follow the tracks of that thoughtless Anglo Tommy Kerns.

Kerns took a sip of his hot coffee and set his cup aside, feeling warm. He smiled at both Mary Agnes and Travis Boone. He was glad he had slipped the Pitchfork loop and located Boone and Mary Agnes. When daylight came, he had already told them, he planned to point his horse toward Texas.

"You ever seen Texas, Travis?"

Boone shook his head. "Never made it that far south."

Boone sat on a ground blanket he had unfolded and laid out another blanket, unrolled, to make a bed for the night. Mary Agnes was placing extra firewood close by to use during the cold, early-morning hours. She did not see the shadowy figure emerge from the darkness outside and take form at the mouth of the cave.

Kerns was squatting by the fire with his hands out over the flames when a shattering shotgun blast ruptured the night's stillness.

Kerns grabbed his side with his left hand and reached for Mary Agnes with his right, shoving her violently off her feet and out of the line of another blast. Kerns lost his footing and pitched over onto his back.

Instinct rather than quick thinking sent Boone out of the glow of the fire, his revolver coming up fast and firing all in one swift motion. More shots, pistol shots, cracked and cut through the air. Suddenly a man in a big sombrero and a long black coat with a fur collar came to his feet and ran low, disappearing into the late-night darkness.

Boone sent a shot at the silhouetted figure and waited for

a return shot. Nothing came. The shooter had escaped. Boone stood up and with caution walked outside. There were tracks and blood. He realized he had not missed as he thought he had. When he returned to the fire, Mary Agnes was crouching over Tommy Kerns, who was flat on his back, dangerously still, his chest smeared a deep red.

The coffeepot had caught a share of the shotgun blast, its contents spilling out. Kerns fought to sit up, holding his right hand against his rib cage. Blood foamed through his fingers and streaked down his side. He looked like a dying man. He hadn't taken a full blast, but what he had taken was enough to put him out of action, maybe permanently.

Mary Agnes stood up. "He's hurt worse than he thinks, Travis."

"The Mexican . . ." Kerns spoke weakly.

Mary Agnes made him as comfortable as she could. She placed a rolled-up blanket beneath his head and uncovered the wound in his side and examined it closely. She found, to her surprise, at least eight puncture wounds, each one showing dark red.

"I've never seen such a wound from a single gunshot," she said, showing Boone the tiny red marks, widened with Tommy Kerns' blood. "What is this?"

Boone looked closely at the wounds. "Nail heads."

Kerns had not moved. He lay on his back, grim-faced, looking weak. A flurry of wind scattered a thin blanket of snow and sleet into the mouth of the cave. Boone removed the coffeepot from the ashes and built another fire. Despite the fire, the cave had cooled quickly. He broke several more sticks and piled them into the flames. He handed Kerns' rifle to Mary Agnes. "I want you to sleep with this rifle at your side. And use it if you have to."

She nodded, taking the rifle and watching him unfurl the heavy buffalo coat. "What are you doing?"

"I'm going after the Mexican," he said.

"No! Wait! Please!" She caught her breath. "Please don't go! You can't find him! It's too dark!"

Boone led the Appaloosa to the front of the cave. He turned and looked at her and said, "If he makes it off this mountain, ma'am, we're done for. He'll go straight to Gorman, and they'll be all over us come daylight."

"It's my fault," Mary Agnes cried. "Without me you'd find your way off the mountain without any problem."

Tommy Kerns sat up. "Don't worry about us," he said to Boone in a voice barely above a whisper. "I'll watch out for Mary Agnes."

"Please, Travis," Mary Agnes begged.

Boone shook his head. "I'm sorry it has to be this way. You wait for me," he said. "No matter what you hear. I'll be okay. There's no sense in me sitting up here waiting for Gorman and his men. They need to know I'm still in Wyoming . . . and still alive."

"Please!"

Then, without thinking of the consequences, he grabbed her by her shoulders with both hands and kissed her full on the mouth. The sudden realization of what he had done hit him like a kick in the belly from his own horse.

He disappeared quickly into the shadows.

"Why?" Mary Agnes asked. "Why is he like that?"

Tommy Kerns stared at her across the fire, his youthful face grim. "It's something he has to do, ma'am," he answered. "He knows what he's doing. Don't you worry, he'll find the Mexican, and then he'll go after Gorman and his men one by one."

Chapter Twenty

Juan Joaquin sat in the dark, badly wounded. He was not a fearless man, and not knowing how long he could remain hidden, he was just moments from becoming a terrified man.

A random shot from a wild man had nearly taken his life. And then he had not found his horse where it should have been tethered. Frightened by the sudden gunfire, the horse had bolted in the wrong direction and was lost.

He had been a fool, rushing in, eager for the money he would have earned for killing the man Gorman hated. He had ignored the three horses at the cave.

And he had shot the wrong man. Travis Boone was still alive!

He shivered violently. A fire was his only chance to survive the night, but a fire could also turn out to be a disaster if he was being followed, as he figured he was. A small fire would help keep the chill from settling into his bones, but it wouldn't be strong enough to drive out the chill in the air.

If he had killed Tommy Kerns, then that gringo Travis Boone had put the bullet into his shoulder. And why wasn't

Boone out here? Was he afraid to leave the white woman with a dead man?

That would be a fool's move, he admitted to himself.

The snow was still falling; he had to hope his tracks would not be discovered.

Tonight he had to rest and do something about the wound—at least put a cloth to it. The bleeding was not nearly as bad as before, but the pain seemed worse.

All around him the land was mostly a ghost dressed in white and completely uninviting. With luck he had found a small overhang among the larger trees, well hidden from above and below. The land sloped, dropping away in a sheer fall into a deep black hole. He was on the edge of a deep chasm.

He examined the wound, then cleaned the blood away with a handful of snow. Luck was true to him. The bullet had taken only the flesh, missing his ribs, and was not as bad as it had seemed.

High up on the mountain, along a winding animal trail, Boone remained perfectly still. He knew that the Mexican would be searching for a place to hide so he could care for his wound. How badly he was hurt, Boone had no way of knowing. And until now he had heard only the wind moving among the tree limbs.

His horse had a loose rein and had picked his way through the mist of shifting snow and over the narrow animal trail while Boone looked for any blood spots in places along the outside of the trail, once riding upon a deep footprint, then another.

He halted the Appaloosa back in the trees, dismounted, and let the horse stand easy. He heard a stone break loose and drop without noise into the darkness far below him. Suddenly, briefly, he thought he heard a man's groan. Other sounds came to him out of the darkness below, but he was unsure from where. Then the wind brought him the odor of wood smoke drifting upward from below, possibly from the valley.

Someone had made a campfire.

Joaquin lay hidden beneath the small overhang. He heard men's voices and smelled smoke from somewhere below. How should he get their attention? He'd yell. Maybe the wind would allow his voice to break through the silence. No. He couldn't do that. Travis Boone would hear him. It would be suicide to even try finding his way down the hillside, and if he yelled, it would give away his position. He moved out from under the overhang and peered down into the dark vastness, unable to sort out any shadow, and then, out of the corner of his eye, he thought he caught a flicker of light deep below and shadows moving about. Then, as quickly as they appeared, they disappeared.

Despite his better instincts, he shouted. "Help! Up here!"

A tree branch cracked in the cold.

Another snapped under the weight of clinging, damp snow. Then it was very still, ungodly still—an icy emptiness in the dark. The overhang was tiny and dirty, yet it did offer some sanctuary from the cold, so he returned to it and crawled as far back beneath the protruding rock as he could. The chill was seeping into his wound.

He dozed. Sometime during the night he awoke. Before his eyes could adjust to the darkness, he sensed he was not alone. His small fire was burning stronger than it should have. Someone had piled it with thick tree limbs. A calm voice came to him out of the darkness.

"Your fire was dying."

Large hands reached out and took him by his belt and pulled him bodily from the hole, jerking him harshly to his feet—a tall man with shoulder-length hair, well over six feet and appearing even larger in the heavy buffalo coat he wore.

Kicking and swearing, Joaquin was carried to the very edge of the darkness. A sudden burst of cold air swept up from below. It whipped at his feet as they hung over the edge of the deep, dark abyss.

He struggled hard to breathe, but the hands that held him never surrendered their grip. They were like steel bands. Suddenly they relaxed, and he was released, falling breathlessly, twisting helplessly, a long, long way down the dark chasm.

Chapter Twenty-one

Wells Gorman was up early. He found the body draped over a large boulder and in the pale light recognized it as Juan Joaquin. That the Mexican was dead meant that he had failed, just as Carter Sims had sworn he would. Which meant only one thing: Travis Boone was still alive!

The night had been long. He had not moved from the fire except to add some wood. It would be another two hours before full light. The dugout they were in was large, shaped with a wide mouth carved out of the hillside by nature. It smelled like a grizzly.

The sky had darkened, and it had gotten colder.

Carter Sims walked over and stared at Joaquin's body. "Well, so much for the world's best tracker," he said mockingly.

Gorman shot Sims one of his angry glances. "He was stupid. He should've warned us."

Sims shook his head. "How could he warn anybody? He was tossed off this mountain like a bale of stale hay!"

Gorman swore. He didn't give a damn. "Boone will pay for every man we've lost! He can count on it!"

"Damn, Wells, nothing's going to change," Sims said. "It seems each time we find where Boone's been, we also find a dead man. I'm telling you, he's stashed that redhead, and now he's bringing the fight to us, just like I said he would. His kind of man will take a lot of killing before he's finished."

"We'll cut his trail sooner or later."

"What about Mary Agnes? How do we find her?"

Gorman didn't answer.

Sims sighed deeply and dug into his coat pocket for the makings of a cigarette. His eyes swept the hillside, squinting through the grayness midway up the mountain.

Gorman saw him staring at the massive hillside and asked, "Is there something I don't know?"

"Just thinking. Maybe it wasn't him."

Gorman turned to face Sims, standing stiffly and looking disgusted, as he had been doing a lot of for the last month. "Well, somebody was up there. The Mex didn't leap off that cliff all by himself."

"I'm sorry, boss. I don't think Boone's anywhere near this part of the mountain," Sims continued. "By now he's either gone back to where he took the Canfield woman, or he's miles off, while we're fiddling around like a bunch of tired dogs. He won't outright attack us. If anything, he's looking for stragglers. That's his style. He'll take one out here, then he'll find another and take him out, until all that's left is you and me and a couple of saloon drunks."

Gorman glared at Sims. "I've got men waiting back there. Good men. When I give the word, they'll be all over this mountain. If Boone's anywhere near, they'll know his every move."

Sims didn't answer.

Gorman added, "If you're so scared of him, you can go back to the ranch and clean stalls!"

"That ain't what I'm saying, Wells. Had Boone wanted, he could have killed any one of us while we slept. He knew we were holed up down here like a bunch of ticks. That's why he tossed the Mex down here. He wanted to let us know he could handle anything we threw at him."

"Just shut up for a while," Gorman growled. "We'll head back after we finish scouring this end of the valley."

Sims had one final say. "Well, as I've been saying all along, this man's a serious mistake on our part. He's got us following a trail of dead men."

"That's enough of that talk," Gorman said. He swung up into the saddle. "We'll ride on a ways. I know of some animal trails up ahead. Maybe we'll find some sign that tells us Kerns is out here on his own. If we don't, we'll turn around and return to the ranch."

Boone smelled the smoke before he spotted it coming from the valley. *A campfire,* he thought. That meant someone had built a cooking fire. He pulled up on a windblown rock overhang and sat in his saddle, expecting to see a couple of Gorman's men hunkered around a fire despite the drizzle.

He pushed through brush to peer at what he first thought was a stagecoach, but upon closer inspection, at a distance of about a hundred yards, he realized he was staring down the mountain at a crudely built camp wagon. A most unusual camp wagon.

Someone had built a war wagon with four tall wooden

walls made into a windowless cabin of sorts. Two rifle barrels poked through a small opening in the wall on his side. No telling how many holes were on the side that faced the mountain.

He was amazed, to be truthful. The tall, tin chimney of the structure puffed dark smoke, rising into the early-morning grayness. A thick-bodied man walked around the horses and relieved himself. On the wagon's side facing him, Boone was barely able to read two crudely printed words: PITCHFORK PROPERTY.

A stakeout.

How convenient. He should have known to expect something out of the ordinary. Though he had no idea how many men were inside their little homemade citadel waiting for him to show himself, he did know he could take care of the wide man before any of the others could pile out of the wagon fast enough to see where the shot came from.

He stood off from the Appaloosa and reached back for his Winchester rifle. Those men weren't down there waiting for the snow to melt, he told himself. They were there because Wells Gorman had told them to be there.

The rifle felt good against Boone's shoulder. The distance was no problem. The wagon could not have been more than ten feet from a small creek running along the mountain's base and into a line of young trees.

By now the drizzle had turned to a steady rain. The small winding creek was already over its bank and splashing against the wagon's wheels. As thunder rolled in the distance, Boone took aim at the man who had relieved himself in front of the horses. But just then, he saw another man in rain gear emerge from the wagon through an opening behind the seat and leap to the ground.

He watched the second man unhitch the two horses and lead them around the rear of the wagon and down to the stand of trees, out of his sight. The man returned and climbed back into the wooden fortress, out of the rain.

Boone turned his attention back to the first man, who stood with his back to Boone. Boone had him clearly in his sights, but he lowered his rifle. He had never killed a man who hadn't had a chance to fight back. The portly man finally turned for the wagon and climbed from the wheel hub to the wagon bed in front of the driver's bench. For some reason he stood looking around, as if he had remembered something he had left behind.

Boone's first shot punctured a ragged hole in the wagon's chimney. Two following shots, in quick succession, brought the chimney down and over on its side, almost splitting it in half.

He could hear loud cursing. The man standing on the wagon seat had fallen to the ground and was crawling for a spot beneath the wagon that was out of Boone's sight.

A man's head appeared from the small opening in front of the wagon, just behind the plank seat, and lost his hat when Boone sent a bullet six inches from his head into the open door, almost knocking the door off its hinges.

Inside the crude contraption, someone had a rifle and was poking the barrel through the small opening, firing blindly, obviously unaware of what part of the mountain Boone's gunfire was coming from. Four more men piled out of the wagon into the rain, hitting the muddy ground and running for tree cover. The wagon had caught fire. Black smoke billowed and swelled. Orange flames erupted and spread across the cabin's roof and along the wagon's sideboards.

Three more shots from Boone's rifle pounded the thick

boards that lined the side of the wagon, ripping splintered holes in the crudely printed letters. A man rose up from the far side of the wagon and was on the run, pulling a coat over his shoulders. He made it a couple of steps before tripping over his own feet and stumbling facedown in the muddy slop that had formed around the wagon, but when Boone didn't fire at him, he was back on his feet and streaking for the stand of trees where the horses were tethered.

A man yelled, "He's here!"

There was no other sound except the single shot Boone put into the ground behind the man up ahead. It stuck in Boone's craw to actually miss and have to watch any man bought by Wells Gorman get away without a bullet hole in him somewhere, even if not fatal, but these men were all afoot in the rain, the wagon was on fire, and as far as Boone could tell, their horses had slipped their tether and were probably halfway to the Pitchfork range.

A grim smile touched Boone's lips. At least the hired guns were getting plenty wet.

Chapter Twenty-two

Having not heard from Travis in two days, Mary Agnes reached a decision of her own, a decision she had been dreading but one she knew she must make, and soon, if Tommy Kerns was going to live through the week.

She had to get Tommy off the mountain and somehow to a doctor. It was that simple. With that in mind, she went to the front of the cave carrying the Winchester, as Travis had taught her.

Outside, she stopped and peered down along the trail. Nothing moved. Tree limbs sagged under the weight of the morning snow.

Travis had been so intent on instructing her. She remembered what he had told her about the trails on most any mountain, in particular mountains such as these: *Follow the curvature of the mountain itself, and ride very, very carefully. Remember, mountain trails have soft outer edges in this kind of weather and will fall away under the weight of a horse if it gets too close to the edge of the trail.*

Kerns was awake, but he was barely strong enough to

raise his head. To Mary Agnes, he appeared no better today than he had the day he was shot by the Mexican, yet she had not heard a complaining word from him. She heated some water and let it come to a boil, then put a steaming cloth on his wounds and hoped it added some comfort.

Finally, taking up the ax Travis had brought with him from the ranch, she left the warmth of the cave again and walked a few feet to a cluster of lodgepole pines, strong and straight.

The ax was sharp, and several quick chops let her cut two long poles and then some smaller branches, which she hastily trimmed of their twigs. She dragged them into the cave and cut notches into the two poles so she could fit the smaller limbs into place, lashing each side with long leather strings she had cut from Kerns' saddle. She went back outside and found heavy pine boughs for the cross pieces, to be weaved tightly with pieces of rawhide cut from her own saddle.

She then folded two blankets and spread them over the pine boughs. She'd read how the Cheyenne Indians, and especially the Sioux, had, before horse culture, used dog travoises when they moved from camp to camp. But it had been Creed, her husband, who taught her how to lash the poles to the sides of a saddle and use a horse to pull a travois.

With Kerns secured on the travois, she led his horse and her pinto out of the cave and started down the narrow trail Boone had taken. From time to time she halted to rest the two horses and to check on Kerns.

"I'm fine," he would say each time. "Don't you worry."

He seemed okay, but his face was as pale as the patches of sky showing through the heavily forested mountain hillside.

"Don't move so much," she said. "You need to lie still."

She had no worry with the pinto. The horse was as sure-footed as any she had ever owned. Kerns' black was a young horse, surprisingly strong, and handled the travois with ease. She had expected that getting Tommy safely onto the travois would be extremely difficult, but it wasn't. He was so much lighter than he looked, and he was now sleeping soundly.

When the sound of two gunshots reached them, Kerns raised himself to his elbows and somehow drew his revolver from its holster and held it weakly at his side.

"That a signal for somebody?" he said in a strained whisper.

"Yes," she said.

The gunshots came from somewhere up ahead, fired close together—six-shooters, by the sound. She thought at first it could have been Travis letting her know he was still alive.

"We need to rest," she said.

Kerns lay silent. The black was tiring.

She had just pulled to a stop on a wide place in the trail when she heard angry voices. She swept the Winchester out of its sheath and in the same movement was on the ground beside her horse, staring back up the trail she had just ridden past. She braced herself against the wind, her feet set wide for balance, the rifle butt solid against her shoulder.

The first man she saw rode slowly toward her, waving his revolver, his lower face covered with a dark scarf. Two other figures followed him, barely discernable. Beyond that she detected other movement, which meant there were more of them, all in a single line and closing the gap between her and them.

The one waving the handgun stopped suddenly and stared right at her. "I got her, boss! I got her in my sights!"

His words had barely died out when she fired her rifle,

not directly at the man's thin body but close enough to nick and frighten his already nervous horse. Then things happened exactly as Boone had said they would. The rider went from sitting in his saddle to clinging to the horn for dear life as the horse's two rear hoofs slipped off the trail and kicked and struggled to remain on solid ground. Other riders were having their own problems controlling their horses, as they rode up on the man desperately trying to control his.

Kerns attempted to bring his gun up to shoot into the crowd of men and horses but fell back onto the travois, helpless. Mary Agnes triggered another shot from the rifle. This time she sent the bullet streaking straight to its target, striking hillside rock and whining off in shattered pieces of lead. Suddenly the ground along the trail gave way to the struggling hind hoofs of the frightened horse. The tall, gaunt man with the handgun disappeared over the trail's edge and plunged out of sight, his scream dying slowly.

Kerns was finally able to raise himself, but he clung to the travois with both hands as the black tried to bolt. Mary Agnes grabbed its reins, bringing the animal to a halt.

"They're gone!" she shouted.

"That was great, ma'am," Kerns gasped. "You took 'em out of the fight before they could catch their breath. They won't try that again. We're safe for now."

Chapter Twenty-three

Travis Boone sighted down the barrel of his rifle, with the butt hard against his shoulder. He had long ago had an open shot and was confident he could take out both men before they would be able to make it to their feet or locate him as high up on the mountainside as he was.

After a few moments he lowered his rifle. It'd be like shooting two fish in a tin bucket. He knew they were Pitchfork riders, not by name but by association. The man who carried a left-handed gun was tall and slender. He looked about thirty, maybe a bit older, and appeared to be the calmer of the two. His partner, Boone guessed, a chubby man who seemed nervous and in a hurry to ride out of there, had a face like a frog. His name was Lonny Nash.

Earlier, Boone had watched them turn and ride away from Gorman's crew a mile north. He had decided to follow them instead of Gorman. They had had some conversation with Gorman, and by their actions he knew they were being told to ride back south.

It was obvious they were sent to find Boone's trail, but

when he heard them talking about breaking loose from the Pitchfork, he decided to wait. If they broke off the Gorman leash, that would suit him just as well. And then he wouldn't have to take the chance of Gorman hearing his rifle fire.

Boone had only seen these men once before, when he spotted them riding with Gorman earlier and with Carter Sims later in the day. He could have taken them both out, along with Sims, at any time he chose, but that wouldn't have accomplished much. He needed to keep Gorman and his men guessing. As long as he could keep Wells Gorman on the move, Gorman wouldn't have time to call all his men into a pack and send them swarming over the mountain like a pack of wild dogs on the hunt for blood.

Slowly, Boone, still hidden in the thick hillside brush, urged the Appaloosa down to another ledge closer to the men below. He leaned forward in the saddle. Small bits of the men's conversation reached him as he sat silently, his rifle handy.

They were discussing their future.

"He's here," the slender man, Clay Fisher, said. He turned to stare toward one of the many rock overhangs that appeared along bare ground. Nash squinted with him. "Where? I don't see him," he said.

"Don't worry, he's here somewhere."

"Aw . . . Why hasn't he shot both of us by now, then?"

"Well, if we stay here much longer, I wouldn't count that out."

Boone continued to wait.

Although he did not believe the two men below knew how close he was to them, he had the advantage. Though neither of them could cause him anything close to a major problem, it made sense to keep them in his sight and make sure they remained on the valley floor and away from the mountain's many trails.

"What are we going to do now?" Nash wanted to know. "You reckon Boone knows about the fire?"

"He could."

"That was a trashy thing Gorman did."

"Yeah."

"Well, I guess we'll just sit here and wait," Nash said.

"Wait for who? Gorman?"

"Who else?"

Nash stood up. "Well, I've changed my mind. I ain't waiting." Boone moved his rifle from his lap. He watched Nash reach for the reins of his horse and heard him say, "You can stay here if you want. I'm riding out as fast as this nag will take me."

Fisher didn't make a sign to show that he cared.

Nash was already in the saddle, shaking his head. He was obviously in a hurry. "What's got into you? I thought you wanted out same as me."

"I've got nowhere to go."

"You got family in Tennessee, don't you?"

"Not anymore."

Lonny Nash rode out of the shadows of the mountain and pointed his horse across the valley.

Mary Agnes Canfield was kicking herself for not thinking far enough ahead. Tommy Kerns needed his wounds cared for, and he needed a doctor to do it. She hadn't thought to bring clean cloth with her in case someone got hurt. Now she couldn't even remove his bloody bandages and replace them with clean ones.

She *had* thought to bring along more dried beef.

"Where are we now?" Kerns asked.

"We're a long way from nowhere, Tommy, it looks like. We've got to keep going."

"I wish I could help."

"You did, back there." She gave Kerns a piece of dried beef and watched him chew for a few moments. When she turned to move on, she spotted a man leading his horse out of the timber fewer than thirty yards away and stopping at the edge of a small clearing.

She stopped and focused her gaze in that direction. She felt her heart surge—*it was Travis!*

He was standing beside his Appaloosa with his rifle pointed at a man who had both arms stretched above his head. There was a small campfire behind the man facing Travis.

She yelled, "Travis!"

It seemed to take forever for her to find a safe path off the trail and down the mountainside without her pinto slipping and Kerns' black losing him from the travois, but she made it happen.

Again she shouted. "Travis!"

Boone heard her, but he remained facing the tall, slender man, although there was a slight change in his expression. She didn't know the man, yet it was an easy guess—Boone had cornered a Pitchfork rider.

Clay Fisher, his hands high over his head, watched Mary Agnes Canfield appear from behind Boone with a man on a travois. The woman was pretty, red-haired, but it was the man on the travois who caught and held Fisher's attention.

Not so long ago that man had stood with him during a fight at Medicine Bow, long before the two of them were hired on at the Pitchfork.

The woman was smiling, yet there was exasperation in the way she stood facing Boone, who was talking to her in a very serious manner.

"Why'd you leave the cave? I asked you to—"

"It couldn't be helped, Travis," she interrupted him. "Tommy was getting worse. He was having fever dreams. I couldn't do anything more for him. He was going to die if I didn't find help."

"I heard shooting up there," Boone said. "What happened?"

"That was Gorman's men."

"They were on the mountain?"

"Yes. They found us, but we escaped when some of their horses slipped off the trail," she said.

Tommy Kerns was awake. He made another effort to raise himself to one elbow and twist his body so he could see Boone. And then he saw Fisher. He stared at him in astonishment.

"Clay! Is that you? What on earth are you doing here? I thought you'd left the Pitchfork."

"I just did."

Boone, looking around at Tommy, made an impatient gesture with his rifle. "You know this man, Tommy? Who is he?"

"Yes, sir. I rode with him. He's Clay Fisher."

"A Gorman rider," Boone said.

"Well, yes, sir, but as a regular," Kerns said. "He helped me out of a bad spot once. . . . He's a good man, Travis, a good man to have on your side. What's he doing out here?"

"He was sent here by Gorman."

Kerns lay back down, his voice cold. "When did that happen, Clay?" he asked.

"Take my word for it, Tommy. I had no intention of shooting nobody," he answered. "At first it was a good job for a man from Tennessee. But when all this mess with the Double Deuce started up, I set my mind on getting out."

"He's no killer, Travis," Kerns said, his voice failing. "We could use him—"

"For what?"

"He knows this part of the country."

Mary Agnes left Kerns' side and put herself between Boone and Fisher. "I'm for keeping him, Travis. We surely need some kind of help. There's nowhere safe for us. Gorman's men are scattered all over. And we need somebody who knows all about Gorman and his men. How about giving this man a chance?"

Boone shrugged. He turned back to stare at Clay Fisher. "I'm not sure we wouldn't be borrowing more trouble."

"We've got plenty already," Mary Agnes said. "Any more won't make a lot of difference."

Fisher took advantage of their conversation. "She's right. I *can* help you folks," he said. "I had planned on riding out of here with Nash but didn't figure that would work. Gorman would have put my name on his list to be shot before the sun set."

Boone lowered his rifle. "What do you have in mind?"

"If you're interested, I know a place we can hide for a while. Couple hours' ride south of here. Place called Cougar Canyon. We could make it before the storm gets any worse if we push."

"Who's there?" Boone asked.

"A man and his Indian squaw. An old friend named Jacob Ames. Knew him up on the Bitters. He'd be glad to have some company, and I'd be proud to take you there."

Boone sheathed his rifle. "All right. But, for now, I'll have my eyes on you."

Fisher stuck out his hand. "I don't have any problem with that. I'll do the same," he said.

Boone took Fisher's hand and felt the pressure of a firm grip.

Mary Agnes reached out and hugged Travis. Then Boone unhitched the travois and boosted Kerns onto the saddle of the black, glancing briefly at Mary Agnes when the move brought a sharp yelp from Kerns.

"He'll do fine. The travois would only slow us."

"The trail's not half bad," Fisher said. "But we need to take care of what's behind us. Gorman and Sims . . . they know about the place we're going, but I doubt they'll come looking this far south right yet. Right now I figure they're on their way back to the Pitchfork after losing your tracks. They'll wait for this storm to break before they come looking again."

They rode in silence for the better part of an hour. Once, when they were on a switchback, Fisher slowed his horse.

Boone caught up. "What's on your mind?"

"That fire up on the Deuce."

"I heard," Boone said, surprising Fisher with his calmness.

Behind them the weather worsened.

The cabin was of an unexpectedly good size, well built, with notched pine logs chinked with mud and plenty of dried moss.

Someone inside had a fire going.

Suddenly the door swung open. A white-whiskered, stumpy man holding a Whitney three-trigger double-barreled shotgun bounded out into the open, hunched over and ready to blast away. "All right, you bunch of varmints, you keep your distance or I'll blow ye clean off them horses!" he yelped. "You hear me? Keep your dang distance! Who do you think you are to come sneakin' in here like a gang of horse thieves?"

Fisher yelled out, "It's me, Jacob."

"Me, who?"

"Clay Fisher! You're acting like the Regulators are still looking for you for what you did up on the Bitters! Simmer down some."

Jacob Ames straightened and peered at Fisher with quickened interest. "Well, I'll be a hound dog, ain't none of your business who I got looking for me! The real question is, what's a Wells Gorman rider doin' up here? This is my place. Now, who are them you got with you?"

"Friends, Jacob. We need some help. I'm not riding for Gorman anymore. This here is Travis Boone and Mary Agnes Canfield. Mary Agnes owns the Double Deuce."

"Who's that man on that little black?"

"Tommy Kerns. He needs some tending to."

"All right, all right, keep your dang britches on."

Jacob responded to the sound of a woman's coarse voice from inside the shack, threatening to smack him on the head with a stick of hickory if he didn't close the door.

"Shut up!" he shouted over his shoulder. "We got us some company, woman. Put some durn clothes on and get some pillows out so we can lay this hurt man on 'em!"

Other than a table, some chairs, and a pile of furry animal

skins, the only other entity in the cabin was the woman sitting on a stool in front of the stone fireplace.

"This here's Woman-of-the-Herbs," Jacob said, winking broadly. "She's part Ute and part Kickapoo."

Woman-of-the-Herbs was dressed in a loose-fitting, one-piece deerskin. She must have weighed in at around two hundred and fifty pounds. Her round legs were fitted tightly into short leggings from ankle to knee, held there by bright red-beaded garters.

Ames stared hard at Boone. "You that feller what's been giving Wells Gorman a bellyache? Well, good fer you, mister. Somebody should've jailed that sorry devil years ago when he first showed."

Boone was still concerned about Clay Fisher. He stood off to one side, watching as Fisher and Mary Agnes very carefully laid Tommy Kerns onto one of Ames' animal skins. The ride along the narrow switchback trail had taken a big share of Kerns' strength, and he was having a difficult time remaining conscious.

"He asked for you," Mary Agnes said to Travis.

Boone crouched beside Kerns. The young man's eyes were cloudy and unfocused. "Travis?" he whispered hoarsely. "I'm sorry to die on you like this when you could use my help, but don't you worry about Clay. . . . He's a good man, Travis. If he said he'll be with you . . . then he will."

"That's fine, Tommy. Now you lay back and rest."

Jacob Ames had been watching and listening with intense interest. Without a word, he dug into a pile of rags on the floor and came out with a clay jug corked with a corncob. He gave the jug to Woman-of-the-Herbs.

"This here's some rum . . . got a Missouri mule kick to it. Give the boy a shot," he said.

Suddenly Woman-of-the-Herbs whispered to Jacob, one bushy eyebrow raised high. Jacob said, "She says your friend looks mighty poor lyin' there like a speared jackrabbit. She can make good medicine."

Woman-of-the-Herbs took up the lamp, and, with the corked rum jug held against her huge breasts with one hand, she went over to Kerns and put the rum jug aside. Next she brought the lamp over so she could see his face.

"He has many wounds," she said in good English.

"Any dang fool kin see that," Jacob growled. He shook his grizzled head. "Tend to 'im, dang it! I done seen enough shot-up men to know that if they ain't dead when they's hit, it's a good sign they'll live to be shot again."

Woman-of-the-Herbs handed the lamp to Mary Agnes, then knelt beside Kerns, humming to herself. She removed his heavy coat, folded it up neatly and placed it under his head, and then tore away the bloodstained shirt, all the time telling him he had a beautiful body.

She brought a rolled-up animal skin and placed it beside him, making a face at Jacob.

"Stop that dang smiling, an' git to plugging them holes in that little feller's body!"

In the dim light Woman-of-the-Herbs fumbled among the tangle of dirty-looking roots that had been wrapped in the animal skin, examining each one closely before choosing from among them.

"Tea," she said, and she handed some roots to Jacob. "Make boil good. It good to heal."

She splashed rum into a large tin cup and forced half of it into Tommy's clenched mouth. He gagged and tried to spit it out, but she held his mouth closed with a meaty palm pressed against his lips. She waited until she was certain he had swallowed the last drop before repeating the process again and then again.

Finally Kerns turned his head to the side, rum spilling onto his chest. His eyes closed, and more rum bubbled out.

"Plenty good sleep," she purred. "Now is the time."

As they watched anxiously, she probed with a large needle into each flap of reddened skin. Mary Agnes hadn't been able to remove many of the nail heads because they were buried too deeply in Tommy's flesh. Kerns stirred at the first jab of the needle, and Woman-of-the-Herbs used one meaty arm to keep him from squirming. Blood dripped freely from the wounds as she dug deeper. When she was finished, she bathed the raw, red-stained flesh with a syrup-like oil from some kind of green leaf she had crushed.

"Dang it, let him catch a breath!" Jacob squealed.

Over by the fireplace, Mary Agnes was stirring the root tea as it came to a boiling brownish color, nodding and smiling at Woman-of-the-Herbs. She knelt beside Kerns and gently poured the tea onto the open wounds.

Woman-of-the-Herbs smiled and started her humming again. She drank a cup of the rum herself before placing a damp cloth across Kerns' forehead.

"He has fever," she announced. With that she stood up and placed a bearskin over Kerns, then another. "He sweat good," she said.

Shortly after midnight, the snowstorm made its way into Cougar Canyon. Only Boone was still awake. Woman-of-the-Herbs lay curled up next to Kerns, snoring and breathing as heavily as a hibernated grizzly would.

In the shed in back of the cabin, the horses were restless. Boone listened until he could hear only the scratching sound of tree limbs brushing across the cabin's roof and the heavy snoring of Woman-of-the-Herbs. He left his bed on the floor, drew on his gun belt and buffalo coat, and walked outside.

It was cold and dark. He could see the horses from where he stood. They were fine. For an hour he stood alone, occasionally brushing the snow from his coat sleeves. Travel was out of the question. It would be a month or longer before the trails would open.

Tommy Kerns was on the way to recovery and also becoming restless, but Woman-of-the-Herbs worried about his thin little body and peaked look and wouldn't allow him to move an inch without her hands being all over him, rubbing and soothing.

For three days she smothered him as if he was her own, bathing him from toe to hairline. "Good man," she would say over and over. He ate very little during those days.

Jacob Ames ate mostly dried meat he had hanging on the rear wall of the cabin. At other times he sat cross-legged, his back to the fire, watching the others finish off fresh slabs of fish.

"Dang smelly stuff, fish," Jacob growled. "Ain't fit for human eatin'."

Woman-of-the-Herbs giggled at him. "Old man act like stupid Crow, don't eat fish."

"Yah, I should've taken up with a Crow woman. They don't talk so blame much."

Fisher was gulping down the last of the fish on his plate. He looked up, alarm showing on his face. "What's wrong with fish?"

"Nothing's wrong," Mary Agnes said, smiling broadly. "Crow people believe fish to be unclean. They say the fish is a cousin to the snake."

"That's too bad," Fisher replied. "Lots of Texans I know live on snake."

Two more days passed quietly.

The storm left a foot of snow on the two hillsides. The third day the wind shifted more to the east, and there was evidence of melting snow along the waterline of the creek. Snow dropped from the gnarled limbs of the pine trees.

It was not a day to be out.

Jacob Ames was roaming his part of the canyon despite Woman-of-the-Herbs threatening to toss out his fish dinner. "This's a fine place for a man who ain't needing much," Ames said to Boone, who had followed him outside to take a look around the canyon. "All ya need is a good woman to give you a bath, cook ya some eats, and let you have some—"

"How long you lived here?" Boone asked.

"I figure must be 'round two years, at least. I was living up there in the Bitters with another squaw when I got myself in a tangle with the Regulators and had to get out 'fore they strung me up to one of their hanging cedars."

Cougar Canyon was a freak of nature, Boone decided, and perfect, with its deep half-circle canyon and no rear outlet. The canyon walls were mostly bare of any vegetation, except for a scrubby overhang that protruded over the cabin's roof like the thumb of a giant hand.

"You expecting Gorman anytime soon?" Ames asked.

"We could leave before that happens," Boone said.

"That ain't why I asked," the old man growled. "I jest wanted to know. If'n there's gonna be a good fight, I'm gonna be doing my own shooting, you know. That Gorman ain't no friend of mine."

Chapter Twenty-four

After being awake most of the night listening to Carter Sims' fitful snoring, Wells Gorman returned to the Pitchfork as disillusioned as a man could be. He was cold, tired, and disgusted. He'd lost more men than he could count. Alvin Albertson was dead, robbed and killed by his own men. Now he had lost Tommy Kerns, Clay Fisher, and Lonny Nash too, and somebody had shot holes in his camp wagon and sent four of his men scampering to other parts.

Of course, he knew who'd done the shooting.

And he still had no canal. His reservoir would soon be nothing more than a huge mud hole. He needed Mary Agnes Canfield out of his way, dead, or in his kitchen.

He went outside and walked straight across the porch and then returned to the house's main room, slamming the heavy oak door behind him. He jerked open a cabinet door, took out a bottle of prime Kentucky sipping whiskey, poured himself a healthy drink in a coffee cup, and downed it almost without taking a breath, savoring the raw sting in his throat and the sudden warm glow in his stocky body.

He had never felt so confused. *How long does it take to kill one bronco peeler?* He stared bleakly at the empty cup and thought of how empty his life had become.

This was a terrible land he lived in, such a violent, hard land. Those who had survived before him had taken from others by force and then killed to hold on to each precious inch of it. Why was it wrong for him to do the same?

All he knew was, a man had to force his way upon others if he was ever going to prosper. That's the way the world was built—by taking from the poor and defenseless.

Carter Sims entered the room with a man sporting a bandage around his head, red stains still showing dark just above his left ear. Gorman downed his second drink. He looked at the bandaged man and grinned.

"Mary Agnes do that?" he asked.

Without waiting for an answer, he dismissed the man. His purpose in life had not changed. He could still order men around. But if he was going to continue being the big dog in the fight, he needed to end this thing here and now, even if he had to kill Travis Boone all by himself. His men had proved to be miserable failures.

"Are we about ready, Carter?"

Sims nodded. "Anytime you are."

"Boone has made a fool of us, you know," Gorman said bitterly. "All we've done is step over our dead. I've made too many mistakes," he said. "That foolish woman. She was my first mistake. And then she hires Boone. Hate to admit it, but I was dead wrong about him. I thought he would break and run like all the others."

Sims had been rolling a smoke.

"Now that Fisher's disappeared, I don't have a man left who's worth a week's wages," Gorman growled.

Sims' face reddened. "Well, I'd say Boone's holed up in Cougar Canyon."

"You mean in there with that old devil Ames?"

"Yes, sir. Has to be. We found their tracks, and they sure didn't head back north."

"Cougar Canyon? How would Boone know of that place? Even Mary Agnes . . . she wouldn't know."

"Fisher."

"What's Fisher know about Cougar Canyon? He's from Tennessee."

"He may be from Tennessee, but he knew Jacob Ames from up in the Bitters. They were longtime friends. Hillbilly people. Them are the kind what stick together like a bowl of grits."

Gorman was a bit cynical. "Well, that don't mean they can't die." He had heard of Cougar Canyon, but never once had he stepped foot inside it or paid it any mind. "What makes you think Fisher took up with Boone? Nash rode off, didn't he? The two of them were together when I sent them to the south end. He could've gone with Nash."

Sims shrugged. "I don't remember us finding Clay's carrion laying around. And we didn't find but one set of tracks heading west. I think Clay stayed behind and rode off with Boone into the canyon—for what reason, I don't know."

"Okay. Get the men saddled," Gorman ordered. "We're going hunting."

It was not yet noon when Boone and Fisher finished their dinner and began checking their guns and gathering ammunition. They left the cabin soon after. Huge dark clouds drifted above them, and a brisk wind blew sharply off the surrounding ridges.

The only thing they heard was Jacob Ames telling Woman-of-the-Herbs to mind her business and get to taking care of Tommy Kerns.

Not long after, Ames walked out the cabin door, frowning and complaining about the snow on the ground. The shooting, he told them, was sure to give his canyon a bad name before another day passed. "It's coming," he said. "I can feel it in my old, creaky bones."

Boone agreed this time. "I'm sorry I brought this on you," he said. "It wasn't my intention."

"Don't matter a dang bit," Ames said. "Way I see life . . . if a man's gonna die, he should do it fighting his tail feathers off. It's good if a man gits to do his fighting with his friends at his side."

Boone knew that all it was going to take was for Wells Gorman to sit down and think about it for a while, and he'd realize he had Travis Boone, Mary Agnes Canfield, Clay Fisher, and Tommy Kerns holed up with no place to run or hide. And now that group of sitting ducks included Jacob Ames and Woman-of-the-Herbs.

Ames snuffed that idea. "This is my canyon," he growled. "Wells Gorman ain't got no right in here!" He held his double-barreled shotgun at his side and watched Fisher and Boone tramp through foot-deep snow, looking for places where they could take cover when the shooting got under way.

Ames turned and looked over his shoulder at Woman-of-the-Herbs, who had come to the door behind him. "You shoot the first man that comes through this door when things get going," he told her. "If'n I ain't back before the moon shows through them clouds, I'd like you to remember all the good times you and me had."

"All of them, Jacob?"

"Well, just pick out the good ones. I'm gonna set my traps right now, so don't do any walking around without me seeing you."

Jacob bounded around the rear of the cabin to a small shed. There he took two traps hanging on a wall peg and brought them with him back around the cabin. One he placed next to a stack of firewood and covered it with a shovelful of snow. The other he placed in the center of the clearing, also covering it with snow that he then smoothed with the back of his shovel.

He stood back and looked at his traps. "Now, you sorry varmints, you come on in here and stick your sorry foot in one of them, and I gotcha in my sights!"

The weather was turning bitterly cold.

Clay Fisher gave all his attention to the lower end of the canyon, where he found some downed limbs and piled them around two large boulders. Higher up, along a bench on the hillside, Boone watched him drag a larger limb filled with brown pine needles and stack it atop the others. It made good sense, Boone thought. Sooner or later they'd need all the protection they could find.

He still had his doubts about Fisher but hoped he was wrong. "How many men you think Gorman will bring with him?" Boone asked him.

"All he can get, plus the cook and dishwasher," Fisher allowed. "Besides that, he'll have Carter Sims and Charlie Evers. Most of the others will be saloon boys looking for a day's pay. I think you've cut a big slash in the regulars. Charlie's been hanging around Six Mile for a week or so. Came here out of Utah. I'd say this would be right up his alley. Thing is, though, he's no spring chicken. Someone said he was blind in one eye. Didn't say which one, though."

"You said Evers?"

"Yeah, that's him—the Abilene Assassin. You know him?"

"Heard of him, that's all."

"Well, he rode in the other day and took up camp in the saloon."

"You saw him? What's he look like?"

"Don't worry, he'll be easy to spot. He wears a red beard, always has, and he's sort of on the skinny side, and he likes to talk to you while he's thinking on how he's going to kill you."

"How much time do we have?"

"I'd say they'll likely be here around dusk . . . one after the other. Gorman's no fool. He'll come in slow and deliberate."

Boone stepped over the tiny creek. He stood there for a moment, wondering about Kerns' condition and Fisher's skill with a rifle. Could he point and shoot? What had happened to Tommy Kerns was a stroke of bad luck. It shouldn't have happened, he thought. Oftentimes, though, it didn't pay to get in the middle of another man's fight. Things seemed to have a way of jumping up in your face when you weren't expecting it.

With Kerns bedridden, it was two against . . . how many? Maybe you could count old Jacob and his bear traps and his shotgun to take out a couple of men without being shot full of holes himself. That might help, but there was still Clay Fisher. How would he turn out?

Truthfully, Boone had to admit he hadn't felt all that trusting of Fisher when they'd first met, certainly not enough to turn his back on the man. But he would find out real soon what sort of a man he had allowed Kerns to talk him into siding with. There was a whole lot of difference between fixing fences, riding herd, and yanking a stuck calf from some gooey bog . . . and being in a gunfight.

A fresh snowflake brushed Boone's cheek and melted.

For the first time since they had arrived at Cougar Canyon, he felt the wind and shivered. He wanted to talk to Mary Agnes but could never find the chance to be alone with her.

He kept his hands warm beneath the heavy buffalo coat, his rifle stuffed under his arm. He had removed the heavy Walker from its holster on his right thigh and thrust it behind his belt.

"Did you see where Jacob put those traps?" Clay asked, shaking his head, his jaw set hard. "We sure need to be careful about those things. We better step lightly and be mighty careful. They'll mess up a man's leg worse'n a pack of wolverines."

Boone agreed. "I pity the man who gets his foot snagged in one of those things."

Walking over the canyon, Boone found it was not as deep and steep as it had appeared the first day they rode in looking for a safe camp, and now that he was giving it a closer look, he thought it wasn't all that beautiful, either.

He had a mind to be a little more conscious of the spacing of boulders and ragged stumps, the woodpile in front of the cabin, the rocks along both of the hillsides, and the downed trees and thick brush. Most of the boulders were within running distance of one another, which might prove helpful.

The small creek was not a hindrance. A man could leap over it or walk through it. Earlier he had found where the stream formed from a spill coming off a ledge beyond the cabin and eventually dropping off into a small sinkhole, where it disappeared to continue underground.

The evergreens grew in lively clusters, thinning out closer to the rim. Ground brush and blackberry bushes were thick in spots, now covered with two inches of snow. To creep in without being seen, Gorman would have to work his way around numerous sharp-edged ledges while keeping low to the ground.

Boone and Fisher were walking around checking out Jacob's bear traps when they caught the whinny of a horse and the sudden smell of wood smoke.

"We'd better take a look," Fisher said.

They climbed the southernmost part of the left canyon wall and stretched out, bellies to the ground. Boone eased forward a few inches so he could peer over the edge for movement below, and he found it. Fisher followed, remaining on his stomach.

A man was hunched over a small fire, less than forty feet away, directly below them. He had five or six horses hitched to scrub brush and small tree limbs. He stood close to the fire, his back to them.

"They've posted a guard," Clay said.

"He's not very happy looking," Boone said. "I don't believe they've made it in just yet, but they're out there and on their way."

"A little early for them," Fisher said with a sigh. "I thought for sure they'd wait till dusk."

The lone man below them was obviously feeling the chilling wind coming hard off the high crags and not enjoying being left behind to tend to the horses. He had his coat collar pulled up above his ears, his hat down low. He kept looking over his shoulder to where the horses nosed around in the snow. Suddenly, though, he was in the saddle of a big bay horse and was on his way out across the valley.

Clay stared after the rider. "He'll bake that bay if he keeps using his spurs like he's doing now," he said, standing and grinning.

They weren't the only ones to observe the man on the bay punishing the horse with whip and spur. Five cloaked riders bunched together across the valley watched also.

Practically directly in line with the constricted entrance into Cougar Canyon, a quarter mile west, Critter Malone, Deputy Pete Judd, the Parker twins, Josh and Jason, and Sheriff Gil Johnson rode up from a draw just in time to see the rider cutting across the valley before disappearing over a rim and out of sight, the setting sun in his face.

Before arriving, Sheriff Johnson had had the group search the lowlands for over an hour. When they found no signs of Boone and Mary Agnes, the sheriff decided they were wasting their time looking that far south. It was his idea to turn around and ride to the Pitchfork, on a hunch that Boone and Mary Agnes had been caught and were being held prisoner until Gorman could find a way to get rid of them.

Critter rode up beside Deputy Judd. "Did you see that rider?"

Pete Judd made a face and said, "Sure did. What I want to know is, where'd he come from?"

"Has to be Cougar Canyon. There's nothing else over in that direction. He must have spotted something in there he didn't like," Critter said. "I figure it was Boone that put him on the run."

"Couldn't be," Judd said. "Boone's never been this far south that I know of. I'm not sure he even knew there was such a place as Cougar Canyon."

Sheriff Johnson moved up to stop beside his deputy. Judd handed him a pair of field glasses. "Take a look."

The sheriff took the field glasses and held them up to his eyes and asked, "You see any other riders around them hills over yonder?"

"No, sir," Judd said. "But that don't mean there's nobody inside that canyon."

Sheriff Johnson handed the glasses back to Judd.

Early that day the two lawmen had discussed places along the mountain they thought Boone would choose. Finding no sign of him after the snowfall, they decided Cougar Canyon was the only retreat on the mountain that would give someone on the run a fighting chance to stand off Wells Gorman and his men.

Critter looked at Deputy Judd rather than the sheriff. "Pete, my gut says Boone's in that canyon, and Mary Agnes is with him."

"You really think so?"

"I do. I don't know how he would have found it, but, knowing Boone, there would be a way."

"If that's true, why didn't we find any kind of sign they were even this far south?"

"The snow. But they're there. I'd bet my life on it." Critter turned to Sheriff Johnson. "Sheriff, I think Boone is already in the canyon, and so is Gorman. That rider we spotted was with Gorman, and for some reason he got spooked. Either that or he was going for more help."

Judd and the sheriff nodded at the same time. "You could be right, Critter," the deputy said. "I'm guessing Clay Fisher for some reason or other took up with Boone and showed him how to get to Cougar Canyon. That's the only answer that makes any sense."

He turned to scan the entire floor of the valley with the field glasses. For a while they just sat in their saddles like statues, each one squinting over the surrounding country-side, waiting for something to move or for someone to tell them what they needed to do and when to do it.

Chapter Twenty-five

Boone and Fisher, inside the canyon and on high ground, were trying to rout a sniper from behind the woodpile just on the yonder side of the cabin.

Keeping his rifle well out in front of him, Boone worked his way along the hillside, pausing and listening, while Fisher edged his way a little lower. "He's not behind the woodpile," whispered Fisher, rolling over onto his left side so he could look Boone in the eye. "He's in that brush off to the right side of it. Can you see anything? I can't get a shot."

Boone didn't answer. He edged his way a little lower on the hillside and settled in behind some rocks, almost directly above the brush Fisher had pointed out to him. Taking off his hat, Boone pushed it up above the rock he was hunched behind. Two rifle shots cracked almost instantly.

Boone retrieved his hat. He found no holes.

"He's there, I think." He pointed the barrel of his rifle across the creek, locating a thicker mass of brush within three or four feet of Ames' woodpile. "He's moved again."

Fisher said. "You're right. I can see his red coat. There's two of them in there, and they can't get out!"

Boone was looking at another spot closer to the creek, where he thought two men were hunched down among low-growing brush. He took a chance and fired one shot into the brush, as if he was flushing it for rabbits. Jacob Ames had been leveling his shotgun at the same spot for more than five minutes, and at the same instant as Boone, he fired both barrels.

The noise was enough to frighten a deaf dog.

Ames stood stiffly. He loaded up, and with a wide swing of his shotgun he fired another blast into a pile of downed tree limbs Fisher had piled up so he would have a workable stockade.

One man, wearing a red coat and holding a repeating rifle, crashed forward and lay still. A second man, hit squarely in the chest by Fisher, followed the first. Fisher was up off the ground and on the move, leaping over boulders and picking his way around a rock pile with the agility of a jackrabbit.

Boone did not have the time to protest. He held his breath as Fisher suddenly skidded to a stop, spun halfway, dropped to his knees, and fired his revolver into the blackberry bushes. Boone scrambled down the hillside and found Fisher squatting on his right knee, sucking air from his short run.

"That took some sap out of my legs." Fisher grinned.

Moments passed as both men remained in a squatting position. "Maybe I can draw a couple out of those bushes for you," Fisher said. "I'll roll over, take a quick shot, and crawl a few feet."

Boone thought that might work. Fisher went for it, and Boone fired from ground level. There was no answering fire.

Then, all of a sudden, a wild scream echoed from the canyon floor.

"Ames got him one!" Fisher yelled across the hillside to where Boone lay.

"Where?"

"The woodpile. There!"

Boone looked. He saw a short man in black britches spring out into the open, but he couldn't go another step. His left foot and ankle were clamped in the bear trap Ames had placed there earlier. He fell flat to the ground, stark against the snow. They could hear him groaning. Fisher began to crawl. Moments later Boone and Fisher both had the man in their sights, but they were hesitating.

"He's in bad shape, Travis."

Boone agreed. Killing a man in the grip of a bear trap could be considered cold-blooded murder. It was not a fair fight.

Ames was shouting. "I'm gonna cut you in two, you lousy scumbag!"

Unfortunately for the screaming man in the trap, killing a defenseless man didn't mean a thing to Jacob Ames, who was standing at a corner of his cabin. This was his canyon. He raised his shotgun, jammed it to his shoulder, and pulled both triggers at the man. The blast spun the man right out from beneath his hat as if he'd been caught by a fence post and sent sprawling over backward, full of buckshot.

It was all over for him.

Fisher shook his head and whispered, "The old man's really hacked off."

Actually, Ames had been hit twice and hadn't mouthed a word. Lucky for him, both shots had only bruised him.

He swung around the corner of the cabin and leaned back against the outer wall to reload.

For a few seconds both Boone and Fisher squatted silently in the grass. They did not discuss their reasons for not shooting a man with a bear trap clamped like a vise around his ankle.

The silence failed to last.

Suddenly three men came out into the open with their backs to the woodpile, rifles at their shoulders, spraying the ground where Ames had been standing when he shot the man in the trap. Fortunately, Ames had somehow made it behind the cabin just as the three men sprayed that corner with raking fire.

Boone stood up. Ames was turning blue in the face as he tried to get his shotgun around the corner for a shot, only to have to duck back out of the men's gunfire.

Boone sent two Winchester bullets into the tallest of the three men and watched him fall over backward and roll onto his stomach against one of the woodpile logs. He didn't move after that.

A short, fuzz-faced man, who had moved off from the other two and was starting to advance on Boone, was knocked off his feet by Fisher's single pistol shot. The last man stood silhouetted with his arm extended. The gun he held pointed directly toward them was empty, but he kept hauling on the trigger as though he meant to die, which he soon did.

Boone turned his attention to a man he had seen hurtling over Ames' bear trap and the man caught in it. He was now on the slope looking down on Boone, who was lying flat on his stomach.

"Look out!" Fisher yelled to Boone, as he fired at the man who had Boone in his sights.

An instant before the man could pull his trigger, Fisher's bullet spun the man around and dropped him to the ground directly in front of Boone.

"That was close!" Fisher yelled while reloading.

Boone shook his head, stared at the dead man, and stood up, facing Fisher, who was gazing at the man lying a foot away.

"Thanks," Boone said.

"My pleasure." Fisher smiled.

Fisher was still standing up in plain sight when Boone yelled and grabbed him by his belt and yanked him back to his knees.

"Stay down!" Boone shouted.

Fisher was still trying to shoot as he hit the ground. Both Fisher and Boone were on their knees as two shots sailed inches over their heads. They spotted the pistol flash coming from a pile of stones down below. Boone, holding his rifle off the ground, aimed at the source of the flash as two more shots rained over their heads.

"I swear that was a piece of good luck," Fisher said. "You saved my bacon there, Travis."

"That's it! The next time you rare up like some idiot, I'll leave you to the buzzards," Boone swore.

Fisher whispered again, "They're on the run."

Boone laughed. He knew better.

Shots were coming from nearby now, mostly thrown at Jacob Ames, who had returned from around the cabin and was standing with his back pushed against the front wall, loading and shooting in all directions. The pistol shots came his way from some not-so-good shooters, their bullets ripping into the chinked logs yet missing Ames and leaving him with time to reload.

Fisher shook his head. "Would you look at that old coot? He didn't even flinch."

But Boone was looking at a man's booted feet sticking through the underbrush into which Boone had just fired, trying to scatter anybody else who might have been in there with the first shooter.

He had one man dead to rights, he realized. The other man had escaped, ducking around the cabin. The last he was seen, he had jumped across the creek and was on his way across the short distance to the canyon entrance.

Suddenly there was a pause in the gunfire.

The wind coming off the ridges ruffled Boone's shaggy buffalo coat. Both Fisher and Boone stood off to one side, reloading.

Fisher looked around. "I think we've slowed 'em a whole bunch, Travis," he said. "We've cut into them more than they thought we could. I'd allow there's some among them wishing they were home in bed."

Boone looked around. Nothing moved. "We haven't seen anything of Evers," he said.

"Well, that don't matter none," Fisher said halfheartedly. "If he's here, we'll certainly see him soon enough."

"I was hoping he'd pull out."

"Yeah. Sure."

Suddenly a shot rang out across the clearing. Somewhere a lone sniper had opened up, and he had selected Ames as his first target.

Boone saw the flash and then saw Ames grab at his shoulder.

"He's hit this time," Boone said.

"Nah. He's just putting on a show so they won't try to shoot again. Look at him—he's hardly bleeding."

The shot had come from another corner of the cabin— one they had overlooked.

"I told you, he's okay," said Fisher. Boone watched as Ames ducked inside the cabin, closing the door behind him.

"He's been a big help," Fisher added. Boone nodded. Fisher pulled his sheepskin coat collar higher on his neck and gazed at Boone. "You know, my old daddy always said it ain't how *many* you got when the fight starts. It's *who* you got."

Boone looked at him and smiled. "Yeah, well, your old daddy was right." Boone paused. "I can't help but wonder why the men that are still here haven't rushed us."

"It'll be up to Sims," Fisher said. "Right now he's probably waiting for us to make a mistake. The little squirt thinks he's in command. He knows there's only you and me, and he's biding his time."

Boone shook his head.

The sky had turned corpse gray.

Suddenly Charlie Evers stood in plain sight, rifle in his hands. "There's no need to be in such a hurry to die," he said. "I'll spend some time with you both before I kill you. So don't worry about little Sims. He's turned tail and skipped out, the little varmint."

Evers stared at Boone. "I'm glad to see you, Alex," he said. "I hear you haven't lost any of your speed. That right?"

"Depends on exactly what you've heard, Charlie."

Boone let his heavy buffalo coat hang open so his gun was clearly in sight. This time it was stuck behind his belt and not in its fast-draw holster.

Boone knew there would only be one distraction that would work against Evers, and that was Fisher, who had moved back a few feet.

Evers continued to stare. Then he brought his rifle up.

Fisher shouted, "Hold it, Evers!"

Evers flinched.

Boone threw himself out of the rifle's line of fire, anticipating correctly. His Walker Colt seemed to leap from behind his belt and land in his palm.

The bullet from Evers' rifle cut through the long hairs of Boone's buffalo coat without burning the skin. Boone's revolver blurred, faster than Evers thought possible. The shot from the Walker, clean and straight, struck Evers in the upper chest, killing him instantly.

"He called you Alex," Fisher said.

"I didn't hear that."

From somewhere up near the cabin, a shot rang out. Fisher grunted and fell to his knees, holding his left leg.

"I should've been sitting," he said.

Ames was out of the cabin again, his left arm in a sling. He spotted Boone and came running, his right hand waving the shotgun in the air. When he saw Fisher tying his handkerchief around his leg and pulling it tightly, Ames asked him, "Who done that to you?"

"It came from over by the cabin," Fisher told him. "You must've missed him."

"Missed him, huh? I didn't even see him." Ames looked at Fisher's leg. "Well, dang, I bet that hurts right sharply, don't it?"

Fisher slowly turned and looked at Boone, shaking his head.

Ames continued talking. "You're a lucky pup, you know. There's a bear trap a foot from your left cheek. You talk about hurt."

Below them, a buckskin-wearing man slipped out from behind Ames' woodpile with his rifle barrel pointed to the ground. To Boone's surprise, the man stared up at them and spread his arms in surrender. He leaned over and carefully placed his rifle on the ground.

Boone stood facing the man. Fisher stood off to one side.

"I'm leaving here, Mr. Boone," the man called out. "And you, Clay. I've sold my saddle this time. I ain't shot no man all the time I been here or pulled a trigger, so if either one of you shoots me, you'll be killin' a man who has a good woman waiting for him, two young kids, a sickly mother-in-law, an' a horse he ain't paid for yet."

Boone held his rifle on the man. "You plan on coming back?"

"No, sir. It's a long ride to Cheyenne."

Boone lowered his rifle and watched the man turn and walk off toward the cave entrance, leaving his rifle behind. Behind him, two more of Gorman's men stepped out from the woodpile and tossed their guns to the ground, then followed the man from Cheyenne.

"There's one man left, Travis," Fisher said, moving up to squat beside Boone.

Boone looked past Fisher. Across the clearing, a man was inching his way like a sidewinder along a jutting rock overhang, inches from the cabin's rear wall, before dropping straight down and out of their sight—and toward the cabin's back door.

"Gorman!" Boone whispered, his heart skipping a beat.

Fisher held out his hand. "Help me up. If you're going in, I'm going with you."

"We can't." Boone was afraid any move he made to break into the cabin would compel Wells Gorman to shoot Mary Agnes or Woman-of-the-Herbs or both. His breath was short, so twice he inhaled deeply and let the air out slowly. He looked at Fisher, who was shaking his head.

"He could kill Mary Agnes," Boone said.

Fisher stared back at Boone. "I know. What are we to do now?"

"We'll wait."

"For what?"

"He's got to come out," Boone said. "When he does, we'll be ready."

Boone and Fisher were bending over Charlie Evers' body when somebody called out for them to drop their weapons and turn around.

"Don't shoot them, men. They look a little ragged."

Boone and Fisher turned to face the voice.

Perhaps ten feet away, Jason and Josh Parker, Critter Malone, Deputy Judd, and Sheriff Johnson sat on their horses, grinning. Sheriff Johnson was the only one staring speculatively at Evers' dead body.

"All right, gentlemen," the sheriff said, "you can start explaining what's been going on around here. Who's that dead man? Where's Gorman?"

His answer came almost immediately.

The door of Jacob Ames' cabin popped open, and Wells Gorman stood with Mary Agnes by his side, his large Army-model revolver barrel shoved up hard under her chin.

Mary Agnes stared at Boone. "He murdered Tommy!" Her voice trembled. "He wants his horse."

Wells Gorman grinned at Boone.

Sheriff Johnson, who held a piece of paper in his hand, his gun still resting harmlessly in its holster, said, "This is a warrant, Wells. You're under arrest."

Gorman ignored the sheriff. He looked at Boone. "Well, well, cowboy . . . look what I've got."

Boone stood absolutely still. His feet were spread apart, his gaze on Mary Agnes. He had little doubt what Gorman had in mind. Mary Agnes was to be his shield. He'd get her onto a horse and ride off with her as his prisoner. Had Gorman planned to kill her, he would have done so the minute he found his way into the cabin. It was that simple.

"Well, cowboy, what's it going to be?" Gorman said with a tight smirk. "You shoot me, or I ride off? Which is it?"

Sheriff Johnson stepped forward. He pointed a long finger at the badge on his coat lapel. "Now look here, Wells. I'm the one who tells you what you can do. I'm the law around here. You're in my territory. Nobody's going anywhere without my telling them they can."

Boone waited. His chance would come.

Suddenly a shotgun hammer fell on an empty chamber, the *clack* sounding loudly in the chilled air. Woman-of-the-Herbs stood in the cabin doorway, staring at the Whitney double-barreled shotgun she held.

She had pulled the trigger on two empty chambers. Ames, in his excitement to shoot and run, had fired the last two shots and had forgotten to reload.

Gorman pivoted, his face pale as well water, still clinging to Mary Agnes with his revolver now shoved against her back. "What th—"

He never finished.

Everything from that point happened quickly. Boone shot Gorman as he turned back around. The bullet, a snapshot, struck Gorman in his right shoulder, knocking him off his feet. He collapsed like a handful of falling poker chips. Mary Agnes was now on the ground as well, having slipped from Gorman's grasp when he'd spun around to face Woman-of-the-Herbs. Gorman struggled to recover, his stubby fingers coiling around his long-barreled Army Colt, bringing it up off the ground and getting ready to fire. Woman-of-the-Herbs was still trying to reload the shotgun.

Sheriff Johnson was yelling.

Boone couldn't wait. He shot Gorman again, this time in the chest.

Sheriff Johnson rushed forward. He stooped down and pressed two fingers on the large, stilled artery of Gorman's thick neck and looked up at Boone. "He's dead. There goes my warrant."

Chapter Twenty-six

It was two days before they'd found all the dead and placed them in Jacob Ames' old freight wagon, one on top of the other, for hauling off to be buried. They buried Tommy Kerns across the creek, on a slight rise in the ground.

Woman-of-the-Herbs cooked Jacob a pan of corn bread and cared for his "pitiful" shoulder with one of her potions. She made Clay Fisher a poultice for his arm.

Sheriff Johnson and Deputy Judd were the first to leave the canyon; they rode out for Six Mile Junction with the sheriff still complaining about being cheated out of serving his warrant on Wells Gorman. Clay Fisher hobbled around looking ill-tempered and asking everybody what they were going to do now that the fighting was over.

It was early evening. The sky was clear. Jacob Ames had cleaned the blood off his bear traps and hung them on their peg in the shed behind his cabin.

Boone and Mary Agnes stood by their horses after cinching their saddles. She raised her eyes to Boone's, looking meditative as her gaze met his.

"Well, we'll need a place to sleep," she said.

"There's the cave," he reminded her.

"I know. It was nice, but I wouldn't want to live the rest of our lives in a cave. Would you?"

Boone took a deep breath. "Absolutely not."

They stared at each other for several moments.

"We could build a log house," Mary Agnes suggested. "There's plenty of good trees nearby . . . and later we could build a big porch. Of course it might take a lifetime to make it good and comfortable."

Boone nodded. "I've got at least the rest of the winter."

"I'm willing."

She walked around her pinto to face him, her blue eyes blinking back tears of joy. Boone reached for her, and with a peaceful sigh, she settled herself in his powerful arms.